"Sometimes impulsi

"I never considered ~~that~~ her head and studied him with a bemused purse of her lips.

"Of course, being impulsive wouldn't be a good business move, but I think trusting your gut instinct is something else entirely."

"Do you think my gut instinct is telling me to say yes?" she asked in a contemplative voice.

He must've been giddy, because he could swear there was a double entendre in her question. "Hell, yes."

She raised an eyebrow and a Mona Lisa smile appeared and disappeared from her face. "I like your confidence, Mr. Song."

"Thank you. And please call me Colin."

"Colin," she said slowly, as though tasting his name on her tongue.

Said in that low, sexy voice of hers, it was a miracle he didn't groan out loud.

"I'll take that into consideration, Mr. Song."

* * *

Off Limits Attraction by Jayci Lee is part of The Heirs of Hansol series.

Dear Reader,

Since I was young, I've always been drawn to the allure of books and movies—the glamour, the romance and the escape. What's not to like, right? In *Off Limits Attraction*, the final installment of The Heirs of Hansol, I combine two of my favorite things to bring you the story of Jihae and Colin.

Writing this book always put me in a playful mood. Something about the two of them and the fun and glitz of their world got me carried away. I so hope *Off Limits Attraction* carries you away to another world and lifts your spirits high. We need that escape more than ever.

As always, it's a privilege to have you choose my book. It is bittersweet to say goodbye to the Song family, but they will be in my heart always. Thank you for accompanying me on this journey. And here is to many more book adventures.

With love,

Jayci

JAYCI LEE

———

OFF LIMITS ATTRACTION

HARLEQUIN

DESIRE

HARLEQUIN®
DESIRE™

Recycling programs
for this product may
not exist in your area.

ISBN-13: 978-1-335-20951-1

Off Limits Attraction

Copyright © 2020 by Judith J. Yi

This edition published by arrangement with Harlequin Books S.A.

For questions and comments about the quality of this book, please contact us at CustomerService@Harlequin.com.

Harlequin Enterprises ULC
22 Adelaide St. West, 40th Floor
Toronto, Ontario M5H 4E3, Canada
www.Harlequin.com

Printed in U.S.A.

Jayci Lee writes poignant, sexy and laugh-out-loud romance every free second she can scavenge. She lives in sunny California with her tall, dark and handsome husband, two amazing boys with boundless energy, and a fluffy rescue whose cuteness is a major distraction. At times, she cannot accommodate reality because her brain is full of drool-worthy heroes and badass heroines clamoring to come to life.

Because of all the books demanding to be written, Jayci writes full-time now and is semiretired from her fifteen-year career as a defense litigator. She loves food, wine and traveling, and, incidentally, so do her characters. Books have always helped her grow, dream and heal, and she hopes her books will do the same for you.

Books by Jayci Lee

Harlequin Desire

The Heirs of Hansol

Temporary Wife Temptation
Secret Crush Seduction
Off Limits Attraction

Visit her Author Profile page at Harlequin.com, or jaycilee.com, for more titles.

You can also find Jayci Lee on Facebook, along with other Harlequin Desire authors, at Facebook.com/harlequindesireauthors!

One

Jihae Park nodded even though she couldn't hear a word Rotelle Logistics's CEO and CFO were saying over the din of the helicopter. The two men were fighting to put an arm over her shoulders to lead her away from the gales blowing from the propellers. Ultimately, they both grabbed a shoulder each and rushed her into the building.

She huffed impatiently as the two men continued to fight for her attention. Her father's people behaved so ridiculously around her. What would they do in the presence of the almighty Chairman Park? They would probably freeze and pop out an egg. Or they would throw out their backs, bowing so low that their noses bumped their knees. The second option was a definite possibility, but the first one was so much more amusing to imagine.

In Los Angeles, she was more than the daughter of Rotelle Corporation's chairman. She was the hardworking and competent vice president of Rotelle Entertainment, and was respected by her employees. She wasn't *just* the chairman's daughter.

She exhaled and drew back her shoulders. She shouldn't get herself worked up. It wasn't worth it. She was probably jet-lagged from her flight to New York last night, and the helicopter ride to New Jersey had been a bit bumpy.

"It's a tremendous honor to have you with us, Vice President." The CEO spoke in Korean once they were inside, bowing ninety degrees at the waist. *Well, what a nob.* The bowing was fine, but the CFO, a US native, clearly didn't speak Korean.

"I'm glad to be here," Jihae replied in English, giving Mr. CEO a pointed look.

She generally didn't mind these visits to various subsidiaries of Rotelle Corporation. It gave her a chance to show them that their contributions mattered. What she did mind was the fact it took time away from her work at Rotelle Entertainment. Luckily, she had competent employees who could cover for her during her trip.

But her father might not be as fortunate with Mr. CEO. He'd been transferred to the New Jersey office from Korea and would sit as the CEO of Rotelle Logistics as long as he remained in her father's good graces. Unfortunately for him, her father couldn't care less about Jihae or her opinions, so the ass-kissing was wasted on her.

Rotelle Corporation had been founded by her great-great-grandfather soon after the Korean War. Its revenue, reputation and political power had grown exponentially until it had become what it was now—one of the biggest conglomerates in Korea with businesses in various industries including food, pharmaceutics, biotechnology, entertainment, media and logistics. She probably missed one there. Yes. Home shopping. She didn't know why she kept leaving that one out.

"Would you be amenable to a quick tour of our office, Miss Park?" Mr. CFO bowed repeatedly to her with prayer hands like a Buddhist monk.

Why do people do that? Jihae wasn't even certain where the custom originated. Did it belong to a country or a religion? She'd only seen the prayer-hands-and-bow thing during yoga and at Buddhist monasteries. When people randomly bowed to her that way, she felt mildly confused and quite offended by the caricature of Korea's culture of bowing at the waist, which was a show of respect used to greet others or to thank them. And it didn't involve bowing ten times at once like an unhinged marionette.

With a resigned sigh, Jihae smoothed her hands over her pristine white suit and schooled her expression into a polite smile. The two men were irritating her to an inch of her life, but there was no need to let on.

She survived the office tour led by the two bickering executives and ate an overpriced meal that didn't come close to filling her up. After acknowledging their hard work and their important contributions to Rotelle Corporation, she bid them farewell.

Despite her assurances that she could find her way back to the roof without assistance, both the CEO and CFO followed her up to say their goodbyes. The CFO repeated his frantic bowing and the CEO held his ninety-degree bow the entire time it took her to board the helicopter. Once the helicopter took flight, they switched to waving so enthusiastically that their hands blurred. They soon disappeared from sight.

Jihae sighed and settled back in her seat, relieved to be finished with her latest heiress duties. The flight back to her hotel in New York City wasn't long, but she had a hard time staying awake. The remarkable view that revealed itself as they approached the city saved her from falling asleep, and possibly drooling, in the pilot's presence. That would've been very un-heiress like.

The helicopter came to a smooth landing on the hotel roof, and Jihae rushed to the privacy of her room. By the time she let herself inside the presidential suite, she was exhausted and starved. After kicking off her snake-print stilettos, she made a beeline for the hotel phone.

"Yes, Miss Park." Her butler picked up on the first ring.

"Could you send up a double cheeseburger with extra jalapeños, some curly fries and three bottles of ice-cold lager?"

"Do you have a preference for a specific brand of

lager?" he asked with his usual fake not-so-British accent.

Jihae had lived in the UK for close to a decade and it was obvious her butler never had. But she would never burst his bubble. If he got a kick out of using a British accent on the job, then by all means, why not let him speak with a fake accent?

"Anything local is fine. Surprise me."

She hung up the phone and took stock of her evening. Her schedule was gloriously empty. Since she didn't need to leave her suite until tomorrow morning, she headed for the bathroom for a proper hot soak. The food wouldn't arrive for at least thirty minutes, and she was dying to scrub off her makeup and let her hair down. Literally.

Princess Jihae, as the Korean media called her, hadn't been born into this world. She'd been meticulously created by the Park family's PR specialist and stylists when the real Jihae was about seventeen. Her parents needed a persona worthy of being a part of their pseudoroyal family—the almighty *jaebul*. She had preferred the prior seventeen years of neglect by them compared to the constant reminders of her responsibilities to her family and the importance of maintaining a perfect image.

By then, she'd already been tall, close to her current five foot eight. They couldn't work the lovely, delicate-flower image on her, so the team decided she would be presented to the world as the picture of aloof elegance. Other than when she was home, Princess Jihae always wore her hair up in chignons, buns or elaborate updos befitting the occasion. And her entire wardrobe consisted of finely cut clothes in various shades of white—all selected by her stylist during the private shows that fashion designers hosted for her family. She'd fought tooth and nail for her right to choose her own shoes as long as they were appropriately upscale.

People probably thought she wore a billowy white nightgown with a chignon to bed. *Ha!* She plopped down on the couch in her French terry joggers and a baggy T-shirt, and draped one leg over the arm of the sofa. Tonight, she was dressed from head to toe in pink. Unsurprisingly, her home-alone clothes were the colors of the rainbow. And her hair was falling freely over her shoulders, brushed but damp.

She grabbed the remote and raised it toward the TV when a familiar "British" voice said from the hallway, "Your dinner, miss."

"Please leave it outside the door. I'll serve myself when I'm ready. Good night, Timothy," she said in rapid succession. He couldn't see her out of character.

After a slight pause, he replied in a slightly miffed tone, "Very well, miss. Please let me know if you need anything else. Anything at all."

"Okay. Thank you."

When she heard his receding footsteps, she scrambled off the sofa and rushed to the door to listen for the ring of the elevator. She waited ten more seconds before opening the door a sliver to check the hallway. All clear. There were only three other suites on the floor, but she couldn't be too careful.

Once she grabbed the cart, she headed straight for the couch and TV, and opened her first bottle of beer. She closed her eyes and took a long swig of beer. *Heaven.* With one hand, she clicked until she found the channel showing *The Bachelor*, and grabbed the burger with her other hand. The first sloppy bite of the juicy, oozing cheeseburger was probably the best thing that happened to her all day.

By some miracle, she finished her burger without getting any of it on her clothes, and leaned back on the sofa with her second bottle of beer. Her favorite part of watching *The Bachelor* was the commercials. American commercials were so different from the Korean ones. She loved the outrageous humor in many of them.

"Tomorrow on *Hollywood Insiders*," the voice-over bellowed from the speakers, "does Sandy Lim have a new suitor? The mystery man with his arm full of Sandy has been identified as an up-and-coming film producer, Colin Song. We'll tell all…tomorrow."

Jihae set down her bottle on a coaster and lowered the volume. She reached for her laptop and powered it up. A film producer dating an actress always made her a little wary, but she didn't jump to any conclusions. After all, love conquers all.

Oddly, her heart was doing an intense HIIT workout behind her ribs, and she couldn't figure out why. Maybe it was the film producer. He was by far the most beautiful man she'd ever seen. But that was nonsense. She'd only had a passing glimpse of him on the screen. She was just excited about getting back to Rotelle Entertainment business.

They had been making connections in Hollywood and getting a decent lay of the land, but there was still so much to learn. Rotelle Entertainment had some clout in the international film industry through Cannes and other international film festivals, but she was the first to admit that they were newbies in Hollywood.

They'd been searching to partner with a US-based production company to even out the handicap. Ego had no place in business, so she'd asked for help where help was needed. Producing and distributing a successful Hollywood film was not child's play, and Jihae was determined to do a damn good job, which meant she had to find a damn good partner.

Could Colin Song be a potential candidate? Just thinking about the handsome producer made soft trembles course through her body. He was so gorgeous. *Gah.* If a glance at him on TV did this to her, she might spontaneously combust if she met him in person. She would never be able to work professionally with him. He would be too big of a distraction.

But what if his production company was exactly what she was looking for? She should look him up. It would all be for business, of course. She couldn't discount him just because of his good looks. That wouldn't be fair.

Springtime in Los Angeles was a ridiculous streak of one beautiful day after another, and today was no exception. It set the perfect scene for the conversation Colin Song was having with the author Jeannie Choi at a cozy little coffee shop filled with fresh flower arrangements.

"I know you could option your manuscript to another production company or even a studio for much more money, but I believe in your story and your vision," Colin said, his voice rising with excitement. He always got this way when he spoke with Jeannie about her book. "I want you to have maximum creative control of the script and you will benefit from a higher percentage of revenue from the box office, DVD, TV, merchandise and the works. You just have to trust CS Productions and be a little patient for the payout."

"Colin, we've chatted a few times now, and I know we're on the same wavelength," Jeannie said with laughter in her voice. "Honestly, you had me at 'maximum creative control.'"

"You won't regret this." He held her hand in both of his and shook it vigorously. "Thank you for trusting CS Productions."

"I'm taking a chance on *you* personally. I don't want anyone else leading this production. I want you to remain my main contact person until the end. Are we clear on that?"

"Crystal." Colin grinned broadly. He liked Jeannie. She was funny, fair and sharp, and she also had that no-nonsense-mom thing going on. She had three little boys, so she probably couldn't help it. The woman laid down the law and accepted no half-assed crap.

He was delighted to work with her. "We'll need to partner with a studio for the film's theatrical release, but I will always be your point person."

"That's what I like to hear," she said with a wink.

They walked out onto the sidewalk and said their goodbyes. It wasn't even noon yet; they'd had to meet before Jeannie's kids got out of school. *Talk about starting the day off on the right foot.* This was a huge win for CS Productions, a company he'd been dreaming of starting since he was a high-school kid. With this option, more opportunities would open up for the company, and the momentum could move CS Productions out of obscurity.

Founding CS Productions hadn't been an easy road for Colin Song. His first business had been a nightclub in LA called Pendulum. He'd started out working there as a server during college. Soon after graduating with an economics degree, he went on to become a manager. When the owner decided it was time for him to retire, he decided to become a silent partner and gave Colin a chance to buy out a small share of the business.

Colin had sold off most of his belongings and emptied his savings account to buy in to the business. He worked his ass off to grow the business, and bought Pendulum outright by the time he was twenty-three.

His grandmother, the formidable Grace Song of Hansol Corporation, had allowed him to become a nightclub owner without censure—not because she approved of his plan, but because she always stood by family. She didn't approve of his choice, but she'd understood why he wanted to branch out on his own, and succeed through hard work, not through his name and connections. He wanted to be a self-made man who never needed to depend on anyone but himself and prove that he was nothing like his father.

His father was the proverbial trust-fund baby who'd never done an honest day's work. He was too busy burning money on expensive cars and women, and jetting all over the globe. His grandmother, and his uncle and aunt—before she'd passed away from cancer—had raised Colin. He had grown up with his cousins, Garrett and Adelaide, who were more like an older brother and a little sister to him.

He now owned several popular nightclubs in Koreatown and West Los Angeles, and business was flourishing. He didn't exactly have a party-animal reputation, but it was his business to ensure that the real party animals had a good time. That didn't make Grandmother very happy with him, especially since he was running his clubs rather than working at Hansol. But his clubs had allowed him to save up enough money to open CS Productions.

His grandmother, the family matriarch, hadn't given up on Colin's joining Hansol one day. So far, she had him on a long leash, but he didn't know how long she would let him go on like this. No matter how hard he tried to distance himself from Hansol and the Song family name, she found ways to hold on to him. In a way, he appreciated that. He avoided all association with Hansol Corporation in public and kept his identity a tightly held secret, but he loved his family and needed to be a part of it.

He revved his engine and drove out of the café's parking lot with a cheek-cramping grin on his face. Jeannie Choi had optioned *Best Placed Bets* to CS Productions. He could hardly believe what had just happened. They only had three employees so far, including him, but they were a tightly knit group. They had a critically acclaimed TV series under their belt, but this would be their first full-length film. He couldn't wait to tell his team members about the news.

Colin had set up the company in a small office in West LA, and he got there in about forty minutes from the suburbs where Jeannie lived. When he opened the office door and entered like a superhero, Kimberly and Ethan jumped up from their desks and ran to him.

"You won't freaking believe this," Ethan said before Colin could open his mouth.

"Rotelle Entertainment is looking to partner with a US production company for their first Hollywood venture," Kimberly blurted as soon as the words left Ethan's mouth.

"This could put CS Productions on the map." Ethan was practically bouncing on his feet.

"Totally!" Kim shouted. Then she clenched her hands into fists, and her expression hardened in steely determination. "We have to lock this in."

Colin still hadn't gotten a word in. He had very mixed feelings about working with Rotelle Entertainment. Even so, he didn't want to dampen morale, so he added his good news to the excitement. "I have something that could help with that."

Both his employees turned to him with blank eyes, as if they'd forgotten he was even there.

"What was that?" Kim said with a confused frown.

Colin chuckled, shaking his head. "Do you remember where I was this morning?"

"Where you were? You never tell us where you're going—" Ethan gasped. "Jeannie Choi."

"Spill it, Colin. You can't keep us in suspense any longer." Kim looked at him like a puppy hungry for a treat.

"I was keeping you in suspense? You guys wouldn't let me get a word in edgewise."

"Come on, boss," Ethan said. "Stop teasing us."

He sighed in resignation. Hyped up, Ethan and Kim were an unstoppable duo. "She agreed to sign an option with us for *Best Placed Bets*."

Much screaming and a group hug ensued. Colin extracted himself and got down to business. "All right. Give me the coherent version of Rotelle Entertainment's search for a partner. Are they looking in their capacity as a studio, or are they planning to coproduce the film, as well?"

He ran his fingers through his hair and listened to Kimberly's recap of Rotelle Entertainment's search for a production company with whom to coproduce a film, which they would then distribute in theaters nationwide. It was a golden opportunity for CS Productions, but goddammit, why Rotelle?

The Song and Park families had a troubled history.

The chairman of Rotelle Corporation and his grandmother had arranged for his daughter, Jihae Park, to marry Colin's cousin, but the engagement was broken when Garrett married the woman he loved instead. In retribution, Rotelle had orchestrated a corporate espionage scheme against Hansol, nearly causing Garrett to lose his CEO position *and* his wife, Natalie. Colin wholeheartedly despised Rotelle Corporation for that.

But he couldn't put his personal grudge ahead of his duty to his company. CS Productions deserved this chance. Ethan and Kimberly deserved it. Unfortunately, from what he'd heard, Jihae Park was the creative head of Rotelle Entertainment. Perhaps he'd luck out and find that she'd stayed in Korea and sent her second-in-command to the United States.

"What's the catch?" Colin said.

Maybe the Rotelle name made him paranoid, but the deal sounded too good to be true. With a great story like Jeannie's *Best Placed Bets*, and the clout of a well-funded production company and studio, it meant they really had a chance at coproducing the best romantic comedy out there.

"There isn't one. Their VP, Jihae Park, has great ambitions for Rotelle's Hollywood debut, and she wants a production company that knows the lay of the land," Kimberly said with a shrug.

So much for his wishful thinking. If they got the partnership, he would have to work closely with Jihae Park. And often. *Hell.* That was going to complicate things. But that was his problem to deal with.

"We should move quickly on this," he said, head-ing toward his office. "I want our proposal in front of Ms. Park before the end of the week."

"Consider it done," Ethan replied, high-fiving Kimberly. "We got this."

Colin closed his office door and leaned his head on it. No one knew that he was Grace Song's grandson. He had no social-media presence other than for his businesses, and he only attended private family affairs. He shouldn't have to make an exception for Jihae Park and reveal his relationship to the Song family. His family had nothing to do with CS Productions, and he wanted to be judged for who he was, not whom he was related to.

However, if Jihae Park found out who he was, it could jeopardize their project. She would probably misunderstand, and believe that he had deliberately kept his identity a secret from her. People like her believed the world revolved around them, didn't they?

Wait. If he was already taking a risk—why not take another? The partnership could give him an opportunity to find new evidence about Rotelle's role in the espionage. Garrett had had their PI investigate Rotelle when they first got wind of foul play, but there were only suggestions of their involvement. It wasn't enough to prosecute them, especially since their pawn had disappeared to God knew where.

Colin sat heavily on his chair and ran his hand down his face. His meeting with Jeannie Choi felt like ages ago, and the elation of that win had faded into a faint sense of accomplishment. One thing was clear—he wanted CS Productions to partner with Rotelle Entertainment for its success and growth, and for the opportunity to repay his family for all they'd done for him. But he dreaded the partnership for himself. He had no wish to spend long working hours with a spoiled, conniving heiress, and the idea of spying on someone made his skin crawl.

He had a feeling this partnership—if they got it—was going to be a dream come true and a complete nightmare.

Two

"So how many interviews do I have left this week?" Jihae asked in Korean to June, her right-hand woman and a trusted friend.

They were sitting side by side on Jihae's office sofa and having a much-needed cup of coffee.

"You'll be interviewing Colin Song from CS Productions today, and Green Grass Productions on Friday," June said.

Jihae's heart immediately switched into high gear at the mention of Colin Song's name. It turned out the handsome producer and his production company were a good fit for Rotelle Entertainment. Even so, she was hesitant about approaching him because of her obvious attraction to him. But before she could decide what to do, CS Productions had applied for the partnership of their own accord.

She still couldn't help but feel conflicted about the whole thing. CS Productions was a strong candidate. But...why did the man have to be so unreasonably attractive? *Just don't be biased one way or another.* Looks had no bearing on a business decision.

"Just two more to go?" Jihae yawned behind her hand to hide her sudden flush. "Thank goodness."

"You're pushing yourself too hard," June said, eyeing her with concern. "Even for you."

"I know. I know." She rolled her eyes then affectionately bumped shoulders with her friend. "It's just that I've been dreaming of this for so long, and we're finally here in the States, living it. It's hard not to be excited."

"Sure. Fine. Be excited. Just slow down a little. You could still be excited working eight to nine hours a day instead of eleven to twelve."

"Maybe you're right." Jihae noticed for the first time that June had dark circles under her eyes that even her flawless makeup couldn't hide. "Oh, my goodness. You've been working those hours with me all this time. How thoughtless of me. I'm so sorry, friend."

"Don't worry about it. You weren't asking me to do anything you weren't doing yourself. I say that's fair."

"Let's cut back to a sane eight hours a day once the interviews are finished."

"Promise?" June stuck out her pinkie, and Jihae shook it with hers.

With their coffee break over, they went back to work like proper workaholics. Her team had sifted through stacks of proposals and narrowed it down to ten production companies to interview. A few were lackluster and some were promising, and now Jihae was down to her last two interviews.

Her earlier glimpse of him on TV had given her mixed feelings about Colin Song, but she wasn't about to judge him based on a snippet of entertainment news. She would do her utmost to be completely fair. Maybe he wouldn't be as handsome in person. *Yes*. He was probably just very photogenic and looked like any other man in real life.

Her phone rang and brought her wayward thoughts to a halt.

"Yup."

"Mr. Colin Song is here to see you," June said.

"Thanks. Please send him in."

"He's level-ten yummy," her friend whispered almost inaudibly.

"Stop that," she said, fighting a laugh.

Jihae hurriedly replaced the receiver in its cradle and wiped the goofy grin off her face. She walked around her desk with her professional half smile on, ready to greet her guest when he came in.

Her office door opened and all the oxygen was sucked out of the room. Colin Song in the flesh. The video clip hadn't done him justice. He took long strides into the office and stood in front of her before she could get a proper breath in. He wore a sharp suit in a perfect shade of gray with a white dress shirt that showed off his athletic physique. His shoulders were so broad, she wondered if he had all his suits custom-made. She should've said hello about three seconds ago, but he was so beautiful she forgot how to speak.

Oddly, he, too, stood transfixed in front of her, his mouth slightly agape. *Oh, bloody hell.* She must seem completely bonkers staring at him like a goldfish of little brain. She shook herself out of whatever spell held her hostage and extended her hand.

"Mr. Song, it's a pleasure to meet you."

His big, warm hand enveloped hers, making her mind go stark white. Then her knees turned to gelatin when he said in a smooth, deep voice, "The pleasure's all mine."

"I'm Jihae Park. I work here," she offered helpfully. *God.* When he uttered the word *pleasure*, it sounded like it was dipped in copious amounts of butter. So decadent.

"Yes," he said with laughter twinkling in his eyes. "I'm well aware of that."

"Well…yes." Jihae gave herself a mental forehead slap, and forced herself to focus on business. It was her comfort zone. She had to stop acting so weird. "Please have a seat."

"Thank you."

He folded his long form onto a sofa, and watched her with quiet eyes as Jihae picked a seat across from him. The coffee table between them created a much-needed barrier for her brain to function somewhat normally.

"I was impressed by CS Productions's proposal. It

was articulate, and it got straight to the point without flowery, superfluous posturing. I appreciated that. And I quite enjoyed reading *Best Placed Bets*. It was endearingly funny, romantic and heartfelt," she said, relieved that she sounded sufficiently professional. "But I want to hear more about your vision for the story."

"Everything aside, I want this film to be a funny, uplifting rom-com that makes the audience giddy— the kind of movie where everyone walking out of the theater has a spring in their step," he began with a smile that exponentially increased his attractiveness. "I'm also excited about the Korean-American main characters, and the cultural elements they bring to the story. I believe the Asian-American audience will be able to relate to the quirks and humor in those scenes."

Before Jihae could respond, her cell phone trilled from her desk. She shot up from her perch and hurried to turn off her phone. When she reclaimed her seat, her cheeks were burning. "I'm so sorry for the interruption. I must've forgotten to put my cell on silent."

"It's not a problem. We've all done that."

"Thank you." She paused to gather her thoughts. "To continue with our discussion, there have been Korean films, including Rotelle Entertainment's, that have been released in the US. So seeing Asian actors as leading characters isn't as rare as it used to be."

"Those films are stunning works featuring Korean culture, but what we want is to represent Korean-Americans as Americans, not as foreigners who live in this country. Films set in Korea obviously don't accomplish that goal."

"I see your point," she said, nodding slowly.

The passion in his words created a spark of excitement inside her. She would need to research and think further on the issue, but she would love to be part of the movement Colin envisioned.

"This film could add the Asian-American voice to the majority's dialogue. Our journey, the same but different, is part of American life, too. It's like this—the French *mirepoix* and the Creole holy trinity are only one ingredient apart. Both of them have onions and carrots, but the *mirepoix* has celeries and the holy trinity has red bell peppers. They are more similar than different, and the difference isn't a bad thing. They're equally good," Colin said, his hands punctuating his words. She liked his analogy, which she readily understood thanks to her many cooking certificates. "I don't know where that analogy came from, but I'm going with it."

She laughed. "No, it makes complete sense."

"*Best Placed Bets* could be a film that takes America one step closer to acceptance without being heavy-handed and didactic. Nobody wants to be lectured, but I believe everyone wants to understand. This film has the potential to be a dynamic, pivotal work in the industry. And with Rotelle Entertainment's influence and resources, the change could be far-reaching."

Colin Song's energy and intelligence made her pulse pick up speed. His dark eyes glowed with intensity, and he sat forward in his seat, bringing his gorgeous face closer to hers. He had lovely, faint laugh lines in the corners of his eyes. He was someone who laughed often, and suddenly she wanted to hear what his laugh sounded like.

She wished she knew some funny jokes. *Wait. Full stop.* She was acting like a tween with a hard crush—thoroughly awkward and dorky. Even her palms were sweaty. This was blooming ridiculous. She surreptitiously wiped her hands on her pants as she leaned forward to show that she was listening with great interest.

When he shifted in his seat, a waft of his cologne drifted her way, and her eyes nearly fluttered shut. Fresh and woodsy, like he'd hiked through the woods to come to the meeting. It took Herculean effort to keep her eyes from drifting to the muscular thighs that filled his slacks.

Oh, Lord. Her mind did not just go there. Her body was already warm and hypersensitive from his proximity. She had to rein in her attraction. Jihae's reputation was built on her unshakeable professionalism and acute business sense. Lusting after the head of a partner company could tarnish that reputation. Without the respect she garnered, performing her job as well as she had been would become impossible.

Moreover, if this attraction led to…something, her father could take the one thing that helped her survive his scorn and her lonely existence—Rotelle Entertainment. Her work was everything to her. She couldn't forget that. Ever. As long as there was a chance of them working together, Colin Song was off-limits.

"Thank you, Mr. Song," she said in a cool, level voice despite her unsteady breathing, and rose to her feet.

"Thank you for your time, Ms. Park." He extended his hand and she put hers inside it, trying and failing to feel indifferent to his touch.

She released a soft wavering sigh, and his eyes shot to her lips and lingered. *Bloody hell.* This attraction might go both ways. A secret part of her rejoiced at the realization, but the sane part of her shivered with apprehension. It doubled her temptation to test out their attraction, but she wasn't a mindless body. She was the vice president of Rotelle Entertainment.

"I'll be in touch in the next couple days," she said, gently withdrawing her hand.

"That sounds perfect. I look forward to hearing from you." He released her hand and blinked rapidly as though he was trying to get his bearings. Could he tell how attracted she was to him?

With a curt nod, he walked out of her office. As soon as the door closed, Jihae plopped back down on the chair she'd been occupying and pulled her shirt-tail out of her slacks and flapped it rapidly. What in the world just happened to her? She had never been so attracted to someone at first sight. It was a crazy, instant chemical reaction, and she could swear he'd felt it, too.

She shot up to her feet and paced the floor. The temptation to explore these newfound feelings was overwhelming, but her willpower had to be greater. Jihae was excited about what CS Productions brought to the table, and she was very much interested in working on *Best Placed Bets*. But did she have the discipline to make certain that she wouldn't act on her attraction?

Partnering with CS Productions would provide a great opportunity for Rotelle Entertainment's venture into Hollywood. Partnering with Colin Song could mean trouble for her. Big trouble.

Colin was back at CS Productions but he wasn't getting any work done. His mind was too busy replaying his meeting with Jihae Park. He dragged his hands through his hair and leaned back in his chair.

Her beauty had taken him by surprise. He had no business thinking it, but it was undeniable…she was beautiful. He couldn't breathe for the first few seconds in her presence. Her hair had been pulled into a low knot, revealing her long, graceful neckline. Her fair, heart-shaped face looked like cool porcelain, with an expression to match—placid and aloof. Dressed in an all-white pantsuit, she'd seemed almost celestial. Like the elves in *The Lord of the Rings*.

When she spoke with a sexy-as-hell British accent in a warm, husky voice, his libido had spiked like it had been hit with a shot of adrenaline. If that hadn't been enough to throw him off, there was the matter of her shoes. She'd worn a pair of nude, patent-leather stilettos—he was a sucker for women in gravity-defying heels—with rock studs imbedded in a *T* shape

over her feet. It was edgy and hot. Were her shoes—
so different from the rest of her—a glimpse into her
true personality? And…he was analyzing her shoes.

"What the hell is wrong with you?" He wearily
wiped a hand down his face.

It was all Colin had been able to do to focus on
the meeting. But Jihae had conducted the interview
with frank professionalism and respect, listening to
what he had to say with genuine interest. What had
stunned him the most about her was her embarrassment and regret at having her cell phone ring during
the interview. The blush on her cheeks couldn't have
been feigned, and she'd apologized profusely. That
didn't seem like something an entitled, self-absorbed
woman would do.

Colin was confused and enthralled by Jihae Park.
Dislike and suspicion were the only emotions he'd
felt toward her before the meeting, but his first im-
pression of Jihae Park now warred with what he'd
assumed her to be. If he didn't know about the espionage, he would've seen her as a colleague he could
respect and come to like. Since they might end up
working together, having some professional respect
for her wasn't all bad, but it made spying on her even
more distasteful.

In all honesty, his plan to spy on her had never
been pleasant. The idea of sneaking around and glean-
ing information from someone through subterfuge
made him mildly nauseous. Besides, he had no idea
how to go about gathering intel or even what kind of
information would help rekindle Hansol's investiga-

tion against Rotelle. All he had to fuel his plan was his loyalty to his family, and his desire to do what was right by them.

Was he willing to put the film in jeopardy for his family? This partnership would be a huge step forward for CS Productions, and it would open up many more doors in the future. Opportunities like this didn't come along often, and Colin wanted to make the most of it. He wasn't about to unnecessarily risk the partnership if it could be helped.

But if he found concrete evidence of Rotelle Corporation's involvement in the espionage against Hansol, he would have to inform his family. He would do everything in his power to minimize the risk of being exposed and see the project to its conclusion, but he would always choose his family in the end. Even over the film. He just hoped it wouldn't come to that.

A knock sounded on his door, and he smoothed the frown off his face. "Come in."

"Am I interrupting something?" Ethan asked, poking his head in.

"Not at all." Colin sat up straighter in his chair, giving himself a mental shake. "What can I do for you?"

"I think we might be able to sweeten the deal even more for Rotelle Entertainment."

His stomach lurched with excitement and dread. "I'm all ears."

Colin was excited for CS Productions, but the thought of being another step closer to spying on Jihae Park started a throbbing pain behind his eyes.

He just hoped his inconvenient attraction to her wouldn't cloud his judgment in this precarious situation. One thing was for certain: under no circumstances could he act on his attraction her.

They would be business associates and any other relationship between them would be unprofessional. It could adversely impact the partnership and stifle the film's potential. That alone should be enough to nip any interest he had in her. Moreover, she was an enemy of the Song family. He shouldn't be swayed based on a single meeting with her. It wasn't worth the complications.

"You know the screenwriter Charity Banning, who wrote the screenplay for *Never Again Maybe*?"

"Of course I know her. She's immensely talented and her comic timing is perfection. Are you telling me that we have her?"

"Sort of." Ethan adjusted his red-framed glasses when Colin cocked an eyebrow. "She's very interested in *Best Placed Bets*, but after her success with *Never Again Maybe*, her pay rate should reflect that. It would be a stretch to hire her on our budget, but a partnership with Rotelle Entertainment should make things like budgets a nonissue."

"Charity Banning would be a fantastic choice." But Colin wasn't sure if Charity Banning would be a big draw for Jihae Park. She might not have even seen *Never Again Maybe* yet. "Is the movie still playing somewhere?"

Ethan quickly typed into his phone and looked back up in five seconds flat. "Most of the mainstream theaters pulled it last week, but the Shadow Cinema in Santa Monica is still playing it a couple times a day."

"That should work. Thanks, Ethan." An idea formed in Colin's mind. It was bad for his sanity, but good for CS Productions. "Good job getting Charity Banning's interest in *Best Placed Bets*."

"You're welcome," Ethan said with a beaming smile, and returned to his desk.

Colin pulled up Shadow Cinema's website on his computer and purchased two tickets for an evening showing.

His hand hovered over the phone for several seconds. Then, with an impatient flick of his head to get his overgrown hair off his forehead, he snatched up his phone. He listened to the dial tone for two deep breaths, then punched in Rotelle Entertainment's office number.

"Rotelle Entertainment," said the singsong voice of Jihae Park's assistant. "How may I assist you?"

"Ms. Park, please. This is Colin Song."

"Hold, please."

Colin caught himself fidgeting in his seat and stopped himself. He was not some awkward teenager asking a girl out on a date.

"This is Jihae Park."

Her sultry voice hit him in the gut, and he was momentarily out of breath. "Hello, Ms. Park. This is Colin Song and I have news that might interest you."

"Do go on. Please." He grinned when he heard the curiosity in her voice.

"We found the perfect screenwriter for *Best Placed*

Bets, and she's interested in working with CS Productions."

"Oh? What's her most well-known work?"

"*Never Again Maybe*. It's a recent release, just fading from the big screens."

"*Never Again Maybe*?" Jihae's laughter, pitched slightly higher than her speaking voice, rang across the line and raised every hair on his arms. She sounded so carefree and young in that moment. "I love that title. So adamant then…not so much. But I'm afraid I've never heard of or seen the movie."

"That's not surprising since you have so many films to keep track of in multiple countries. I assure you it's great, but you don't have to take my word for it. I found a theater still playing it, and have taken the liberty of getting us tickets for tomorrow night at eight twenty."

"For us? At the theater?" She sounded stunned, and Colin frowned. Did she think he was asking her out on a date? *It couldn't be.*

"CS Productions would like to persuade Rotelle Entertainment to work with us. I believe seeing *Never Again Maybe* will convince you that a perfect story with the perfect screenplay could be ours if you say yes to the partnership."

"Let me have the name of the theater and I'll meet you there at eight o'clock sharp." Her voice was poised and professional once more. "Will that work for you, Mr. Song?"

"Absolutely. It's the Shadow Cinema in Santa Monica. I look forward to seeing you tomorrow."

Colin hung up his phone and placed his face in his hands. He could barely handle a phone call with her without getting hot and bothered. How was he going to keep it together sitting beside her in the dark?

By remembering what a coldhearted, vengeful woman she was.

Jihae Park had planted a corporate spy in Hansol and endangered their partnership with Vivotex, a multibillion-dollar venture. Not only that, but she'd also chosen a spy who had been Natalie's college boyfriend to cast the blame on her, and put Garrett's marriage in jeopardy. How could Colin forget what Jihae had nearly done to his cousin and Natalie? What she had almost accomplished with Hansol Corporation?

No, he could never forget that. Not only would he not forget it, but he would also get this partnership any way he could and get hard, cold evidence of Rotelle Corporation's culpability in the Hansol affair. Somehow. That was what tomorrow night was about—making sure CS Productions secured the partnership for its future and finding justice for his family. He wasn't in any way motivated by his attraction to her.

His argument was so convincing, he almost had himself for a second.

Three

Jihae felt glued to the spot and none of her limbs obeyed her. Had she just agreed to go to the movies with Colin Song? It certainly wasn't a date. People wanted to wine and dine her all the time. This was no different. He was only trying to get in her good graces so she'd partner with his company.

But Jihae had never even been to the movies at a public theater. She'd been sequestered to watch movies in her family's private theater or at the office. It would've been a lonely, isolating experience, but the movies always transported her out of there. She couldn't imagine how wonderful the experience would be with a room full of people. She was beyond excited about going to a real theater. Their home theater served five-star meals and beverages, but she wanted nothing more than some popcorn and a Coke. She wanted to experience the movies as they were meant to be, enhanced by the shared excitement of the other viewers. It was going to be amazing.

She couldn't tell June. She wasn't trying to keep it a secret from her friend. After all, it was nothing. But she didn't want June to blow things out of proportion and call it a date. That was unacceptable. It was a casual business meeting to determine the quality of the screenwriter's talent. It was necessary for her to make an informed decision.

After a short knock, June walked into her office, and Jihae stared at her with wide eyes, not saying a word.

"I've done more research into Colin Song and his production company, and everything comes up squeaky clean and up-to—" June stopped both talking and walking when she looked up from her tablet. "What the heck is going on here? What's the matter with you?"

"Nothing," Jihae replied in a tiny voice.

"Don't even go there. I want you to spill it in five seconds." She began counting off on her fingers. "One. Two. Three. Four—"

"I'm going to the movies with Colin Song," she nearly screamed then clapped her hand over her mouth. When she resumed, her voice was at the right decibel. "It's a business meeting."

"Whoa." June ran the rest of the way to Jihae's desk and sat on a guest chair that faced her. "Is that why he called? To ask you on a date?"

"Are you out of your mind, woman? It isn't a date. He called to let me know that he had something to sweeten the deal. He'd found the perfect screenwriter for *Best Placed Bets*. On that note, I want to know everything you can find on Charity Banning."

"Got it. Now go on."

"I told him I'd never seen anything Ms. Banning has written. He said there was a theater still playing her latest film and offered to take me to watch it. He wants to convince me how perfect the film could be with someone who could masterfully transform the story into a great screenplay."

"All I hear is 'blah, blah, blah.'"

"I'm serious, June. This is not a date. I can't risk my professional reputation by having people believe that I have a personal relationship with Mr. Song. Can you even imagine what would happen if my father found out?"

Her parents would accuse her of being naive and frivolous for dating a colleague, and put her under complete lockdown and take Rotelle Entertainment from her. Sadly, she wasn't exaggerating at all. When her father had agreed to let her work at Rotelle Entertainment, he probably thought she was seeking a fleeting distraction. He didn't believe she'd excel at her job and become recognized as a successful businesswoman. According to him, it made her big-headed and fed her rebellious nature. He would jump at the chance to remove her from her position over the slightest mistake, but she hadn't given him the opportunity so far.

As for her rebellious nature, she had smothered it to ashes after her one flailing leap for freedom. When she'd finished her last term at Oxford, she had disappeared into the countryside instead of attending her graduation. Both of her parents had *prior arrangements*. Couldn't they have made an effort to *care* for once? After all, her college graduation was a huge milestone. Their absence had made Jihae furious and reckless.

Even though she'd lived in Oxford for nearly eight years, Jihae had never been allowed to travel around Europe on her own. She decided if she didn't take a chance then, she would never be able to be on her own, even for a few months.

She'd relied completely on the cash she'd saved up, and had taken Eurail to go from city to city, mostly staying in hostels. It had been the most freeing, exciting few months of her life. She had returned to the UK and settled down at a little inn in the Lake District when her father's men had tracked her down. They'd escorted her home immediately, and she had never been out of her family's and the security guards' sight again.

After years of denying her entreaty to expand Rotelle Entertainment to Hollywood, her father's sudden order for her to travel to the US was a godsend. Her parents' unreasonable expectations and constant scorn had become unbearable to live with. Especially when her engagement to Garrett Song had come to an end. Jihae had been secretly overjoyed by the cancellation of her impending arranged marriage, but her parents blamed her for the broken engagement. For bringing shame to their family. They told her Garrett Song broke the engagement because he'd somehow found out about her selfish, wild nature. Just one, single rebellious incident as a college kid had permanently marked her as the family's black sheep.

"I just wish you could have some normal moments in your life," June said with somber understanding. "You're like Rapunzel trapped in a tower. Even an ocean away, your father controls your every action. Why can't you go on a freaking movie date?"

"Someday, but not with this man. Getting involved with a business associate is unprofessional and improper enough to give my father the excuse he needs to remove me from Rotelle Entertainment."

Jihae reached out and squeezed her friend's hand. It meant so much to have someone who understood that she wasn't living a fairy-tale dream. She was grateful for the privileges she had, but being a *jaebul* heiress meant isolation and loneliness. It was like being imprisoned in a golden cage, tightly leashed at all times.

"Okay. Fine. Then you better make sure no one construes your outing as a date, either. You did mention him being on *Hollywood Insiders*."

"That was because he was with Sandy Lim." She'd almost forgotten that he might still be dating her. Yet another reason not to get involved with him. He wasn't available. "I doubt they'd follow him around when he's not with her."

"You know there are Korean media plants track-ing you in the US, don't you?"

"Bloody hell. Should I just cancel the stupid thing?"

"No. The paparazzi don't get to dictate what you do. It's enough your father has so much power over you. You just have to make sure you look the part of a businesswoman."

"Do I ever not?" Jihae sighed wearily. "But I know what you're saying. I'll make sure and wear one of my pantsuits, not even a dress suit, and low-key shoes. And I'll shake his hand when we meet and as we part. Those will make good, boring pictures."

"You're a pro. But can you try to have a little fun? Just a little bit. Deep inside."

Jihae burst out laughing. "I adore you."

"I adore you, too."

The next evening, Jihae smoothed down her jacket and made sure she didn't have a single strand of hair out of place before she stepped out of her cherry-red Corvette. It was a bit showy, but there was no rule that said she had to buy a white car. When she was in Korea, she happened to be driven around in white cars, but it had never been specifically discussed with her PR specialist.

She was lucky enough to find a spot in the tiny parking lot behind the equally quaint theater. Her sen-sible, white wedge heels clacked against the sidewalk as she strode toward the ticket booth, and it took all her strength not to stop and gawk at Colin Song. He'd ditched his jacket and tie, and he wore a pair of khaki pants and a white button-down shirt with his sleeves rolled past his forearms. Manly, veiny forearms. *Gah*. That multiplied his sexiness tenfold in her book.

Without breaking stride, Jihae came to a stop in front of Colin and extended her hand to him. She braced herself for impact. Even as a frisson traveled down her spine, she kept a polite smile on her face and maintained direct eye contact. But she forgot to withdraw her hand, and Colin didn't seem to have any intention of releasing it. Unable to feign calm a second longer, she took a hasty step back and her hand dropped to her side when he let go.

"I hope I haven't kept you waiting," she said in a steady voice. She was a freaking rock star. No one would be able to tell she wanted to climb all over the man in front of her.

"Not at all. You're right on time. I just got here a few minutes early."

"Did you say you already purchased the tickets?" she asked, not sure about the right protocol for their casual business meeting. It should be fine if he already bought the tickets. He could expense it.

"Yes, I have the tickets," he said, extending his hand toward the entrance. "Did you want anything from the refreshment stand?"

She nodded a little too eagerly. She would finally get to try all the movie-theater goodies. "Yes, but I'll get them myself."

"By all means. I'll stand in line with you."

Colin stood beside her, keeping a respectable distance between them. Very businesslike. Soon Jihae was lost in the wonderland of choices. In the end, she ordered a small popcorn, a Coke slushie and some peanut M&M'S. She peeked over to where Colin was ordering, curious about his selection. He only had a bottle of water and some red licorice. She must look like a junk-food glutton.

Oh, screw it. It might seem a bit unprofessional, but this was her first time at a public movie theater. She was going to live a little.

"Are you ready?" Colin asked, coming up to her. He was obviously holding back his amusement at her bounty.

"No, I'm not done ordering. How are the nachos?" she said and snorted at her own joke. Then she gasped in horror. *Oh, Lord.* She instinctively lifted her hand to cover her mouth, but she was holding her Icee, so she stuck her straw in her mouth and took a long sip. Her public persona had slipped way off at the wrong time in front of the wrong person. She was grateful she didn't get a brain freeze in front of him on top of everything.

"Horrible, but the pretzels aren't half-bad," he answered in a level voice, though he was grinning from ear to ear.

"Shall we?" She arched an eyebrow and bit hard on her cheeks to hold back her answering smile.

"Yes, we're in theater three. There are only three theaters here, so it's easy to get around." He quickly reined in his smile, but his eyes still sparkled with humor.

He led them to their seats in the center aisle and several rows back from the screen. It was perfect, and it was all she could do to contain her excitement. It wasn't until they were seated and the lights went out that she noticed how close they were sitting. He definitely wasn't man-spreading, but he was a big man and his leg grazed her knee when he shifted in his seat. *God, it felt so good.* She really was a sad, lonely woman to get turned on by an innocuous brush of his thigh against her leg.

Before she could spiral into one of her self-pitying moods, the previews filled the screen. She couldn't help but critique the trailers, but she promised herself she would lose herself in the feature film, let herself feel the full impact of the screenplay.

She drank half of her slushie, and ate almost all of her M&M'S and popcorn before the movie started. She hadn't eaten dinner, so she only felt a little guilty. Colin extended his box of red licorice to her, and she took one with a sheepish smile. She was doing a horrible job with her Princess Jihae persona. Was she trying to get him interested in her? No. Not possible. She wasn't hard up enough to risk Rotelle Entertainment for a man. Definitely not *that* hard up. She ripped off a piece of her licorice with her mouth and chewed vigorously. This attraction. It would fade. She would just book a date with one of her vibrators. Some good solo fun would do the job.

When the feature film started, all thoughts of lust and dirty fun were replaced by joy, tears and laughter.

* * *

In the name of all things holy...

Jihae was so close to him that he could feel the heat radiating off her body. She smelled fantastic, and that laugh of hers was doing strange things to his heart rate. And the cracks in her icy demeanor did nothing to cool him down.

It struck Colin that he was sitting beside an actual human being with a sense of humor, empathy and dedication to her work. He couldn't fit her into the spoiled-villainess role he'd created in his mind. Of course, he still didn't trust her, but it had been the idea of her that he'd despised, not the real woman. He wouldn't go so far as to say that he liked her, but he would be lying to himself if he said that she still made his skin crawl. The problem was she made his skin feel tight and sensitive with awareness. He couldn't have those feelings toward her.

His smiles and charm weren't exactly feigned, but he had the partnership in his mind. He had to make that happen in order to earn her trust, and have her drop her guard around him. He cringed inwardly at using her that way, but this was the path he'd chosen. Hopefully, she would let something useful slip.

Colin wasn't going to seduce her—he would never do something that abhorrent—but he would befriend her if necessary. She'd only moved to the United States several months ago and couldn't have made many friends with her famous workaholic tendencies. Besides, he wouldn't be acting based purely on his ulterior motive. If all went well and they ended up working together, they needed to get along to be the most efficient and productive team they could be.

That was why he watched her more than he watched the movie. He'd already seen it and knew Charity Banning was the one, but he wanted to learn about Jihae Park. For research purposes.

Unlike the professional mask she'd worn during their meeting yesterday, her face was an open book. Her smiles brightened up the darkened room, and the tears falling down her cheeks made his chest squeeze tightly.

At the end of the film, Colin knew he had her. She'd watched the movie with undivided attention and reacted exactly as intended in every scene. Rotelle Entertainment wasn't what it was now because of her lack of good taste. Jihae knew Charity Banning was golden. He gave her some time to wipe her tears and gather her armor around her—because his gut told him that was what her ice-queen demeanor demanded—then spoke quietly to her.

"Ready?"

She nodded and he gave her his hand to help her up. He didn't know why he did that, since she obviously didn't need help to stand from her seat, but she was too polite to refuse and put her hand in his again. Maybe he was getting addicted to the sensations that flooded through him whenever their hands touched. Her long, delicate fingers wrapped around his palm— her hand was as soft as silk and just cool enough for him to warm up in his bigger, rougher hand. As usual, her eyelashes fluttered in response to his touch, and he felt his blood rush south.

Colin quickly dropped her hand and berated himself for the impulsive move. But he felt less panicked once they were out in the brightly lit lobby.

"So how did you like the movie?" he asked, already knowing the answer.

"It was just how a perfect rom-com should be. The jokes didn't take away from the tender poignancy of the movie, and the dark moment didn't shrivel up my soul, but made me empathize strongly with both main characters. It's a very well-written, acted and directed movie. Thank you for introducing me to it."

"Don't forget," he said with a teasing smirk. "I have ulterior motives."

Her eyes widened for a second, then she awarded him with a small but genuine smile. "I have to admit you're very convincing. I'm going to consider your proposal very carefully."

"Why not say yes now?"

"That would be very impulsive of me, wouldn't it? If we work together, you'll learn that impulsivity isn't one of my flaws."

"Is impulsivity always a flaw?"

"Yes," she said with a frown, as though she couldn't believe he had to even ask.

"Hmm. I disagree. Sometimes impulsivity can make life more fun." Colin wondered what Jihae would be like if she let down her guard and let spontaneity rule. He definitely wanted to see that. *No, you don't, idiot.* Why did he keep forgetting his objective when he was with her?

"I never considered that a possibility." She cocked her head and studied him with a bemused purse of her lips.

"Of course, being impulsive wouldn't be a good business move, but I think trusting your gut instinct is something else entirely."

"Do you think my gut instinct is telling me to say yes?" she asked in a contemplative voice.

He must've been crazy, because he could swear there was a double entendre in her question. One that turned him as hard as iron. "Hell, yes."

She raised an eyebrow and a *Mona Lisa* smile appeared and disappeared from her face. "I like your confidence, Mr. Song."

"Thank you. And please call me Colin."

"Colin," she said slowly as though tasting his name on her tongue. Said in that low, sexy voice of hers, it was a miracle he didn't groan out loud. "I'll take that into consideration, Mr. Song."

"Oh, yes. You don't want to be impulsive. Right, Ms. Park?"

"No. No, I don't."

Colin woke up the next morning, bleary-eyed and agitated. He'd dreamed of Jihae Park all night and was now painfully hard. She was one of the most beautiful and intriguing women he'd ever met. But he couldn't let his inconvenient attraction to Jihae Park cloud his judgment when it came to the partnership and his duties to his family.

He scrubbed his hands over his face and threw back his covers. He took a cold shower to get his head on straight. Once he was ready, Colin visited two of his clubs and met with his staff. His clubs were well-oiled machines, but becoming comfortable with the status quo wasn't an option. He worked continuously with his managers to move the clubs to the next level.

By the time he checked his watch, it was close to noon. He wasn't someone who flustered easily, but his stomach churned as he waited for Jihae's call. After how she'd reacted to the movie last night, she had to say yes. But she had a shrewd business mind and he couldn't take her acquiescence for granted. The more he thought about it, the more unsure he became about the outcome.

Sitting around and fidgeting wasn't his style, so he headed for Pendulum next. It was the first nightclub he'd owned, and its success had made all the other clubs possible. It was Pendulum that had allowed Colin to move out of his father's house, where the decor had gotten more hideous with each new wife he married, and get CS Productions off the ground.

Twenty-five minutes later, Colin pulled into his parking space at the club and walked inside. He sighed with relief when Pendulum—his place of solace—welcomed him home.

"Hey, Tucker. How's it going?" he greeted his manager, walking farther into the club.

"Everything's going smoothly, As for me, I would

like a month paid vacation," Tucker replied, following Colin into his office.

"You and me both."

"What brings you in? I wasn't expecting you until Saturday."

"I needed to relax," Colin said with a rueful smile, delivering the truth like a joke.

For a brief second, Tucker frowned, as if he wanted to say something. Colin's longtime employee and friend knew something was up, but he chuckled instead, giving Colin the space he needed. "Well, you go ahead and do that while I run your nightclub."

Once Colin was alone, he logged on to his computer to get some work done. The distraction would do him some good. When the lights clicked off in his office, he waved his arms to alert the sensors. He was so focused on the clubs' marketing plans that he must have been sitting like a boulder for the last twenty minutes. When the lights came back on, he rolled his shoulders and returned his attention to the screen.

After his office plunged into darkness for the fifth time, Colin stood up and gave in to the urge to pace. It was late afternoon. Maybe she didn't plan to call him today. But he'd been so certain she was close to a decision last night.

"Damn it," he muttered, frustrated with himself and the whole situation.

Colin continued to disappoint his grandmother by refusing to work for Hansol Corporation, but his love and loyalty lay with his family. They already knew that, but he wanted to do what was right. To protect them and redress the wrong done to them. And, of course, the partnership opportunity would be a giant leap forward for CS Productions. That had to be why he felt so impatient to hear from Jihae Park. His impatience had nothing to do with his desire to hear her voice again. None whatsoever.

His cell phone rang as soon as he finished his thought, and he picked it up on the first ring, barely registering the caller ID. "This is Colin."

"Mr. Song, this is Jihae Park." She sounded slightly winded and his gut tightened with worry. Was she okay? Was she nervous about telling him bad news? But that didn't make sense. Why would she call him to deliver bad news? That was what emails were for. He took a deep breath through his nose and waited. "Rotelle Entertainment has decided to offer a partnership to CS Productions for *Best Placed Bets*."

"That's amazing news. CS Productions accepts the offer. We're thrilled to work with Rotelle Entertainment." His heart was beating hard enough to bruise his ribs, and he couldn't stop the smile that spread across his face. "With the partnership sealed, we can lock in Charity Banning as the screenwriter. We're going to make one hell of a film."

"We certainly are," she said. Her voice held a hint of a smile. "I'll have my assistant email over the contract once we're off the phone. Let's make it official."

"Thank you, Jihae," Colin said in an unintentionally low voice. "Would it be all right to call you by your first name now that we're partners?"

"I believe that's perfectly appropriate, Colin."

most tangible in its intensity. To make matters worse, it wasn't one-sided, which would've made it far easier for her to quell. Knowing he felt the same pull as she did made her helplessly drawn to him.

Helpless. She didn't like the sound of that. Losing control was an unknown to her and she had no interest in going down that road. Considering the potential of the partnership, she'd decided to ignore whatever chemical reaction was brewing in her body to work together with CS Productions. But her phone call with Colin had set her heart racing, and her confidence in her self-control turned a bit wobbly.

Regardless, the decision was made and there was no going back. She ended any chance of exploring their attraction for the privilege of producing *Best Placed Bets*. It was the best decision for Rotelle Entertainment, so it was the right decision for her.

"June," she said into her phone. "When you send over the partnership agreement, could you also schedule for the CS Productions team to meet with our team? They're going to be working closely together. Let's get them introduced sooner rather than later."

"Sure thing. Will you be attending the meeting?"

"No, I don't think I will, and neither should Colin. The two teams should get a chance to know each other in a comfortable environment without their bosses breathing down their necks. It's meant to be a casual meeting where they discuss their visions for the movie, and get excited about producing it."

"Should I make it a lunch meeting? I'll book one of our conference rooms, and have it catered."

"That's a great idea. Thanks, June."

"Anytime. That's what I'm here for."

Jihae replaced the receiver with a smile on her face. Excitement for the partnership bubbled up inside her. *Best Placed Bets* was the first romantic comedy that she would be working on, and she loved the humor, love and heartache the story held. She couldn't wait to see it come together as a feature film—a larger-than-life realization of Jeannie Choi's love story between two Asian-American characters.

Having the honor to work on *Best Placed Bets* came with the heavy responsibility of making a film worthy of bringing the spotlight on the importance of representation. It had to capture the hearts of the viewers and convince Hollywood that they wanted—no, needed—more diversity in the industry. She would work with Colin to make *Best Placed Bets* a long stride in the right direction for his cause, and create momentum for more Asian-American films to come.

Jihae was up for the challenge. So, yes. She'd made the right decision for Rotelle Entertainment and herself. All she could do was hope for their attraction to fizzle out. And soon. Keeping herself in check was only going to get harder the more time she spent with Colin.

Jihae wore a white jumpsuit with elegant silver embroidery across the bodice and on the hem of her pants. Colin stood at her side in a sharp, blue suit with a slim white tie as they smiled and posed for the cameras. They were at an awards ceremony to support Charity Banning's nomination for best adapted screenplay for *Never Again Maybe*, as well as utilize the ceremony to publicize Rotelle Entertainment and CS Productions's partnership.

It was Jihae's first time attending this casual, laid-back awards ceremony held on a beautiful stretch of Santa Monica beach. This was one of the things she liked about working in the United States. It wasn't all about glamour and glitz, but sometimes about down-to-earth fun where the celebrities connected with their fans in a closer, more intimate setting.

After smiling until their cheeks cramped, Jihae and Colin retreated to the huge tent where the ceremonies were being held. She was acquainted with many of the beautiful people, but there were plenty she hadn't been introduced to. It would be unbecoming of Princess Jihae to fangirl over her favorite actors and actresses, but that didn't mean Jihae wasn't sorely tempted to.

"This isn't the kind of awards ceremony that you're used to, right?" Colin asked, leaning close so he could be heard in the crowded venue.

"Everyone seems so much more approachable and relaxed. I feel like I could walk up to just about anyone and talk to them."

"Then do it."

"Don't be silly," Jihae said with a small smile. "We'll say hello to the people we need to and possibly make some advantageous connections as necessary. Remember, I'm the great Chairman Park's daughter. I'm not allowed to gush over stars. That would be undignified."

"That must suck sometimes." Colin looked steadily at her. "Including nights like this."

"It's hardly an inconvenience. I'm quite used to it."

Jihae was surprised and grateful for his empathy, but she didn't let it show on her face. She refused to act the part of the poor little rich girl. "But feel free to mingle. Don't hold back on my account."

"I won't," he said, but he made no move to leave her side.

She was embarrassed at how glad she was that he stayed with her. She needed to stop acting like a fool. Jihae reminded herself that he might be involved with someone else.

"Is Sandy Lim attending tonight?" she asked.

"Sandy?" Colin cocked his head, wearing a quizzical frown. "I have no idea."

"Oh?" Her heart skipped to a happy beat against her will. She didn't care whether he was with Sandy Lim or not. "I saw some speculations about you being her new boyfriend."

"Oh…that." Colin scratched the back of his head with a sheepish smile. "She's a good friend. She needed help keeping her real boyfriend—well, actually her fiancé now—a secret until they were ready to make their engagement public. I was what you would call her decoy arm candy."

"Decoy arm candy?" Jihae laughed. "Well, congratulations on your performance. You obviously did a good job of distracting the public. How long will she need you to play the part?"

"Well, she just walked in with her forever arm candy on her arm, so I guess I'm free of my decoy duties."

"They must be making things public tonight." Jihae turned around to see the beautiful actress walking into the tent with a handsome, glowing man beside her. "They look so happy together."

"Yeah, he's a great guy," Colin said. "They deserve each other."

He almost sounded wistful, as though he was envious of their happiness. Just as she was. Jihae really needed to get herself under control before she built a fairy-tale story for her and Colin.

He didn't have to stay beside Jihae like her bodyguard. It was obvious she was perfectly comfortable in her environment. She greeted her acquaintances with grace and warmth, and introduced herself to new people with poise and confidence. It wasn't because she *needed* him, but because Colin *wanted* to stay by her side. It was as though he was caught in her gravitational pull.

Just as at the movies, he found himself spending more time watching her than the awards ceremony. In the darkened theater, he'd been able to enjoy all her changing emotions without effort. Tonight, out in the open, her serene face hardly changed at all. But he could see the subtle differences in the light of her eyes and the curve of her lips. The ever-changing, dynamic current under the calm surface of her de-meanor held him captive.

"Charity Banning."

He heard the presenter intone as though from far away, but when he saw Jihae bounce ever so slightly in her seat, he realized what had just happened.

"Yeah, Charity," he yelled, clapping furiously for the talented screenwriter.

Jihae clapped beside him, her face as placid as ever, but he knew she was as excited as he was for Charity because she was sitting on the very edge of her seat. When the crowd quieted down, she leaned toward him and whispered, "So well-deserved."

"Yes, and imagine what she can do for *Best Placed Bets*."

"I know. I so hope she will decide to work with us."

"We're close," he assured her.

Colin's blood hummed with excitement. Charity Banning was a gem, and she was going to transform a beautifully told story into an addictively entertaining script. His and Jihae's partnership was already proving to be an amazing match. And he was dying to pull her into his arms in a bear hug, but he didn't think he could handle it.

The rest of the ceremony passed in fast-forward mode as many films received the recognition they deserved and others were passed over. Colin's high remained until the end, and he couldn't wait to brainstorm with Jihae about their joint project.

"Let's go," he said.

He tugged Jihae to her feet, hoping he could convince her to have dinner with him. Her hand felt so right in his that he held on to it for a second too long.

Jihae gave him a soft smile, gently freeing herself. "I feel like I could talk the whole night away."

His eyes shot to hers. He wanted to kiss her so much in that moment that he couldn't breathe. But more than that, he wanted to share his ideas and excitement for *Best Placed Bets* with her. He wanted to know what she was thinking and hoping for. He wanted to know her.

"You want to grab some food?" he asked in a voice much huskier than the question warranted.

"Yes, please," she said, and glanced at her watch. "We need to find someplace that stays open late."

"You've been to Pink's, right?" he said as he got into his car.

"Nope. I've never been." Jihae grinned at him from the passenger seat. "And I don't want you to pass out or anything, but I've never even heard of them."

"Seriously?" Colin shot her a sideways glance, his eyebrows hovering near his hairline. "How long have you been in LA?"

"Eight months or so."

"You've been missing out. Pink's is a Los Angeles institution and you can't call yourself a true Angeleno until you've had a hot dog there."

"Well, we can't have that. Let's go get some dawgs."

They lucked out and snagged a parking spot right outside the hot-dog stand. He'd deliberately chosen the least romantic place he knew—he needed help to keep himself in check—but he didn't want to make Jihae walk for miles in her heels.

"Oh, wow! Is that the line?" Her jaw dropped when she saw the line of people down the street and around the corner. "Must be some hot dog."

Colin grinned at her wide-eyed wonder, proud he was responsible for it. Her excitement didn't cease even after the forty-five-minute wait.

"Ready to order?" the cashier asked when they finally got to the counter. She gave them a friendly smile despite the never-ending line.

Colin turned toward Jihae, who waved him on to order first. Even after studying the menu for nearly an hour, she wasn't ready to decide on her first Pink's Hot Dogs experience.

"Two Planet Hollywood dogs, onion rings and an Orange Crush." Then he turned to her with a raised eyebrow.

"A Martha Stewart dog and a root beer," she ordered in a rush as though she was afraid she might change her mind if she didn't hurry.

"Good choice," he said.

"I hope so." She still sounded nervous about her decision.

"You really can't go wrong with them."

They sat down at one of the white plastic tables with aluminum fold-up chairs and waited for their order. His mouth watered as he watched the other patrons devouring their dinners. It was an elbows-on-the-table, talk-with-your-mouth-full kind of place. He hadn't been sure if Jihae would appreciate a restaurant like this, but there was no doubt she was thrilled to be here. A genuine smile danced in her eyes, the shuttered look of her business persona nowhere to be seen. God, she was breathtaking.

Their dinner arrived and her eyes widened at the sheer size of their hot dogs.

"That's a lot of food." She sounded more delighted than worried.

Without further delay, they dug in. *Damn*. It was heavenly.

"So? What do you think?" Colin waited expectantly for her response.

But she'd just taken an enormous bite—her cheeks expanded like a chipmunk's—and could only nod enthusiastically. After swallowing, Jihae grinned dreamily at him. "Oh, my goodness. The last twenty-seven years of my life have been a total waste. What was I doing when there was food like this to inhale?"

She continued to surprise and enchant him. She took another bite of her loaded hot dog, leaving behind a dollop of sour cream on the corner of her lips. Without thinking, Colin reached across the table and grasped her chin. To his great pleasure, her lips parted on a soft sigh as he gently brushed the pad of his thumb at the corner of her mouth, and her eyelashes fluttered like butterfly wings. He quickly withdrew his hand and leaned back in his seat as though he'd touched fire.

"Sour cream," he choked out.

"Oh." Jihae flushed a bright pink as she grabbed her napkin and scrubbed at her lips. "Thanks."

"No problem," he said with forced nonchalance.

Jihae recovered from her brief embarrassment, and he managed to drive out his lusty thoughts. Barely. They ate in amicable silence, and quickly cleaned off their plates. She ate like she meant it. He liked that.

"*Best Placed Bets* is going to be amazing. I can feel it," she said as soon as they'd cleared the table.

"Charity is going to do an incredible job with Jeannie's beautiful story."

"I know." Jihae sighed happily, then asked in a slightly hushed voice, "Who do you think should play our heroine? I think Sandy Lim is a good candidate."

"Sandy's great, but I think finding someone new and fresh might be the way to go."

"I hear what you're saying, but there are some risks involved there."

"There are risks to everything," he countered with a shrug. He was grinning broadly because he even enjoyed disagreeing with her. The slight tension and the anticipation of how she would respond made adrenaline rush through his veins.

"Of course there are, and taking the *right* kind of risks is essential to good filmmaking." She smiled back at him, seeming to enjoy herself as much as he was. "But maybe we're getting ahead of ourselves. Our future director might have something to say about the matter, too."

"True, and I want us to be closely involved in the location scouting," he said. "There are some scenes in my head that I see so clearly that anything different will feel off."

"I hope our visions are aligned because I have several scenes that are dear to my heart, as well."

They grew silent as they gazed at each other, and their smiles waned. She felt it, too. The electricity hummed between them. This was merely the start of their partnership, and they were going to spend much more time together. They couldn't let every lull in their conversation become charged with desire. *But how do you stop something this instinctive and fierce?*

He coughed into his hand and broke the silence. "We have a lot of work to do tomorrow."

"Yes," she said emphatically, her business face back in place. "Why don't we call it a night? We're going to need all our energy to get this project off to a proper start."

And they were going to spend half that energy just to resist each other. Colin prayed fervently that their attraction was a fleeting thing…not believing for a moment that it was.

Five

With an impatient sigh, Jihae scrolled through her never-ending emails. It was close to six o'clock, the new close-of-business she'd promised June. She had cheated a bit by starting her day at seven, but her friend didn't need to know that.

She pushed away her mouse and leaned back in her chair, drumming her fingers on her thighs. There was no use trying to concentrate with only five minutes left until quitting time. She logged off and stood from her desk. Unsure of what to do next, she paced her office in an agitated to-and-fro. She couldn't understand her peculiar mood. It wasn't only her disquiet at how much of a distraction Colin Song was promising to be, but for the first time, work hadn't been enough to fill her day.

Jihae was discontented and restless. That was why she felt so off. She'd gotten a taste of freedom through her "business meetings" with Colin, and remembered how much she used to long for it—to lead a normal life outside the range of her parents' censuring eyes.

She would indulge in just one more adventure to get the restlessness out of her system. What was something she'd never done before? There were so many things she'd missed out on... What could she do? Then one bright idea lit up in her head.

"June." Jihae peeked out of her office, and motioned for June to come inside. "Psst, psst."

"Quiet. You're making a ruckus," June said, deadpan, not looking up from her computer. Her friend didn't stand from her desk until she'd typed a quick succession of words on her keyboard. Then, and only then, did she stride into Jihae's office. "Now, tell me. Why are you flagging me down like a crazy woman?"

She burst out laughing. June loved teasing her about her reserved manner at work. But her friend would be surprised to know that Jihae felt far from reserved right now. She was craving fun and excitement.

"I want to go to a nightclub."

"You set up a meeting at a nightclub? Why would you do that? Don't those sleazeball businessmen usually take other men to those places to have 'hostesses' sidle up to them and pour their drinks? Ew."

"I never said I had a meeting. I want *you* to go clubbing with *me*," Jihae said rather clumsily. She'd never uttered the words *go clubbing* before. "Not to a Koreanized club. That'll be too risky. More people are likely to recognize me there. I want to go to a hot, American nightclub."

"You—you want to go to an American nightclub? A 'hot' one?" It took June a couple seconds to close her gaping mouth. "Who are you, charlatan, and what have you done with my bestie?"

"Oh, shut up." Jihae blushed, regretting her impulsive request. This was so unlike her. "Never mind. Forget I said anything."

"Oh, no, you don't. You can't back out now." June rushed to her and wrapped her in her arms. "I can't believe you waited until you're close to thirty to rebel against your father a little."

"Hey, I'm only twenty-seven. Besides, I'm not rebelling…" Wasn't she? Was she captivated by a newfound hunger for adventure, or was she lashing out against the punishing rigidity of the life that her father forced on her? *No.* She had found peace with her life, and she counted herself lucky to have a job she loved. "Really, I'm not. I think I'm bored of working nonstop. Of work being the only thing in my life."

"You're finally talking sense. Work should never be your everything. You need to let your hair down and get a bit sloppy once in a while. Where is the fun in being so flawless all the time?" Her friend stood back and studied Jihae from head to toe. "I know the perfect place for tonight. All the staff went clubbing a couple weeks ago—it was your treat, of course— and we had such a great time. I think you'll love it, too. Alas, I can't let you just walk into a club looking like Princess Jihae."

"But all my clothes look like these. Or there are the floor-length dresses. I don't want to draw attention to myself, especially not as a weirdo wearing a white ball gown to a nightclub. My other alternatives are purple, pink or baby blue sweat suits. Even I know that I won't get past the bouncers in those."

"Are you forgetting how filthy rich you are? Your stylist isn't here, but you don't need her. Instead, you'll have your best friend pick you the hottest, tiniest dress you've ever worn. Rodeo Drive is only twenty minutes away."

They rushed to the parking structure and hopped into Jihae's flashy sports car. As soon as her seat belt was secured, June scrolled through her phone until "Oh, Pretty Woman" blared from the speakers.

"You're like Julia Roberts except you don't need a man to pay for your clothes," June shouted over the music.

"Girl power. Woo-hoo," Jihae hooted, and sped toward Rodeo Drive. Everything around her looked sharper and even the air tasted fresher. It was the taste of freedom.

As the theme song of *Pretty Woman* played in a loop in Jihae's head, she tried on every outrageously seductive dress that June piled onto the salesperson's loaded arms. She felt like she was living a different person's life, and it felt wonderful. But distress niggled at the back of her mind. If she loved someone else's life so much, what did that say about her own?

* * *

June wouldn't let Jihae look in a mirror until she'd poked and prodded her for an hour. Thank goodness she was used to being poked and prodded for hours by her stylist. Otherwise, she might've shoved her friend to the ground and run to the streets screaming for help. She couldn't breathe properly in the shimmery silver mini dress they'd chosen, and her butt cheeks were asleep from sitting in the same position for too long.

"There. Go 'mmm,'" June said, smacking her lips together. Jihae did as she was told, hoping that was the last of it. "You're all done, and you're welcome."

"Thank God. I can't feel my bum." Jihae stood from her seat and opened her friend's closet door for the full-length mirror. Her reflection made her breath catch. "I look smoking hot. I'm so glad you sat in on so many of my styling sessions. I think you're even better than my stylists."

June laughed as Jihae twisted this way and that to see all of herself. Her simple, spaghetti-strap dress clung to her curves like magic water, transforming her rather narrow, slender body into a delectable, curvaceous one. Her dramatic cat's-eye makeup and bloodred lipstick made her look bold and mysterious. But her favorite thing about herself right now was the long, jet-black waves that flowed down her back and shoulders. This—this was no princess. No, the woman staring back at her was the mistress of her own life. She did as she wanted and no one could stop her.

"I'll get ready fast, then we'll go clubbing," June said, ducking into her bathroom.

Jihae nodded distractedly and turned her gaze back to herself. She felt as though she had shed a layer of her skin and revealed a hidden side of her. Perhaps her true self. The one that matched her red, patent-leather stilettos—the only thing on her that she'd already owned before tonight. But Jihae knew who she was. Whenever she was alone, she could be as sloppy and goofy as she wanted. But a sudden rush of melancholy hit her. Maybe the real her wasn't a silly side character in her persona, but a powerful, vibrant woman that shouldn't be hidden.

Enough feeling sorry for yourself. This version of her might have some aspects of her true self, but she had to acknowledge that Princess Jihae also held parts of her. Her drive to succeed and her search for perfection had never been feigned.

Her friend stepped out of the bathroom looking beyond gorgeous in her black sleeveless dress. "Let's go party, babe."

With a resolute nod, Jihae straightened her spine and let a wicked smile spread across her face. "I'm ready."

Colin buried his head in work all day, but it didn't do much to distract him from thoughts of Jihae. Immobilized by his conflicting dread and excitement about the partnership with Rotelle Entertainment, he barely finished half of the tasks he'd set out to get done.

He pulled his hand down his face then eyed his leftover dinner with a grimace. The turkey club and fries had long gone soggy, which was just as well since he didn't have much of an appetite. He couldn't figure out why he was so twisted up.

His door cracked open and Kimberly peeked into the office. "Staying much longer?"

"No, I'll probably follow you out in a few," he said, rubbing his temples. "You're here late."

"I was finishing up my research and presentation for tomorrow."

"I'm looking forward to it. Selecting the right director is an essential part of our project."

"Would it be unprofessional to say 'Duh'?" She smiled cheekily at him. "Of course it is, and I'm excited to share my thoughts with you. So go rest up. I want you sharp tomorrow."

"Yes, ma'am."

And just as he promised, Colin logged off his computer and closed shop for the night. It was already past ten, but he needed a drink to wind down, so he decided to head over to Pendulum.

The pressure in his chest eased a bit as he drove his car onto the road. He was letting his emotions get the best of him, and that wasn't like him when it came to business. He hadn't made millions by his midtwenties by being wishy-washy. He laughed wryly at the cocky observation. His confidence hadn't hurt, either.

But now he questioned what was up and what was down. Was Jihae a spoiled villainess or was she a brilliant businesswoman with the allure of an angel?

Who the hell knew? He certainly didn't. *No.* No, that wasn't true. Colin stubbornly tipped the scale toward villainess and quelled his doubts. He had to keep his crap together if he was going to get anywhere in his investigation.

By the time he parked his car at Pendulum, he'd almost convinced himself of Jihae's culpability. All the evidence, albeit circumstantial, pointed to her involvement in the Hansol espionage. Her arrival right at the onset of the suspicious activities, and the targeted attack on Garrett and his marriage, implied that she had been seeking revenge against his cousin. With long, impatient strides, he walked into the club and headed straight for the bar. He planned to down a double cognac then take another into his office to enjoy more leisurely.

"Hey, Tim," he said, waving down the bartender. "How's your evening going?"

"Like a pretty typical weeknight. It's just busy enough for it to be fun, but not enough to make me sweat."

"Then you won't mind if I trouble you for a drink."

"Not a problem. Double cognac?" Tim asked.

"You know me so well," Colin said with a grin.

Something about the music made him turn his head toward the stage and his suspicion was confirmed. Tucker was mixing the songs. He got the complete picture when he spotted the regularly scheduled DJ nursing a beer at the bar.

"Hey, Dan. Did Tucker beg you to sit out for a bit?"

"He's this huge, intimidating dude, right? But he

does a damn good puppy-dog look." Dan shrugged sheepishly. "I can't say no when he pulls that on me. It also doesn't hurt that he's the manager."

"You did good. He misses being up there, and it helps him let loose a little. Managing this place isn't an easy job."

"Yeah. I totally get that." The DJ sipped his drink as his eyes drifted to the stage. He whistled under his breath, shaking his head. "Those two women have been dancing like crazy for the last hour or so, and they're distracting as hell. In a way, I was relieved to let Tucker take over, so I could stare at them properly. They look like goddesses but dance like unoiled automatons."

With a wry smile, Colin turned toward the direction of Dan's gaze and froze. June from Rotelle Entertainment was dancing with a woman who bore a striking resemblance to Jihae Park. The woman was wearing a dress that looked like liquid metal poured over her. It hugged her curves and moved sinuously against her body as she danced. Her dramatic eye makeup and her red pouty lips made her look sultry and enigmatic at the same time.

Whether he could believe his eyes or not, she was indeed Jihae. She was so far outside her brand that she was nearly unrecognizable. He didn't like surprises but he could definitely live with this one. He wondered if this seductive, bold Jihae was closer to her real self than the armor-wearing businesswoman. This side of her made Colin's desire spike even higher.

Goddesses who dance like unoiled automatons. He

chuckled under his breath. Jihae and June weren't the best dancers, but they made up for it with enthusiasm. He admired their complete disregard for what people might think of them, focusing on their joy instead. Shaking their heads, jumping in place, waving their arms...everywhere. Their sheer abandon made them shine, and Jihae glowed like a multifaceted crystal, too mesmerizing to look away from.

When Tucker dragged down the tempo and transitioned into a slow, sexy number, Colin shook himself out of his stupor. He welcomed the break from their dancing. His tongue was on the verge of unrolling out of his mouth, and his heart was already doing its damnedest to shove itself out of his chest. He was turning into a freaking cartoon wolf.

But as he swiveled back toward the bar, he caught a glimpse of Jihae and June stepping closer together. *Oh, hell no.* He swung his stool back to face the dance floor and lost the battle to keep his mouth closed. It was completely innocuous. They were hugging each other and laughing as they swayed from side from side. But the problem was, they were *touching*. No matter how innocent and playful they were being, watching two beautiful women dance and touch was too much to handle. Colin's eyes were threatening to pop out of their sockets.

"Damn," Dan said, and whistled quietly by his side.

Colin had forgotten that he wasn't their only audience. A low growl started at the back of his throat, but he swallowed it with supernatural willpower. He wanted to punch the drooling DJ off the barstool, which was ridiculous since he'd been doing the same thing a second ago. Even so, he wanted the younger man's eyes off Jihae.

"Dan, go relieve Tucker," Colin said in a deceptively casual voice. "Playtime is over."

"But…"

The protest died on his employee's lips when he saw Colin's expression, and he hurried toward the stage. The unexpected surge of possessiveness left Colin unsettled and on edge. He'd dated his fair share of women, but he'd never been the jealous sort. But it was different tonight. He didn't like other men looking at Jihae that way. At all.

After downing his glass of cognac, he strode to the dance floor with deliberate steps. He braced himself for their shock at coming face-to-face with him on their night out on the town.

"Jihae," he said, drawing her attention. "What an unexpected pleasure."

June slowly stepped away from Jihae and stood beside her in a protective stance. Jihae lowered her eyes to her shoes as a lovely flush spread onto her chest, neck and cheeks. After a few breaths, she shifted her gaze to his face, and he couldn't find a trace of her shyness or surprise.

"Colin." She nodded her head in a regal manner that Colin couldn't reconcile with the playful, happy woman he'd seen a moment before. The carefree Jihae was disappearing and he wanted to hold on to her before she could hide away completely.

Possessed by an inexplicable urgency, he stepped close to Jihae and pulled her into his arms. "May I cut in?"

He glanced briefly at June, who exchanged a look with Jihae, then shrugged. "By all means. I'll be at our table."

Jihae watched her assistant—who was obviously a close friend—walk off the dance floor, and met his eyes again. She placed one hand near his collar and drew it slowly down to his shoulder. Then she offered him her other hand, which he wrapped up in his own, and cradled it to his heart. Colin gulped audibly as he placed his free hand on her back and pulled her a little closer. Her soft body fit so perfectly against the hard planes of his own.

"Well, this is rather awkward. It was supposed to be my secret night of debauchery," Jihae said in an even voice that didn't reveal a hint of nerves, whereas he was trembling inside. Did she have the slightest idea what she was doing to him? Maybe he was too late and she'd gone back inside her armor.

"Was it?" he replied in a slightly rough voice. Because he could certainly oblige and assist her with the debauchery. "Well, I think it's a perfect chance meeting to celebrate our partnership."

"By dancing together at a nightclub? Besides, we already celebrated our partnership at the awards ceremony." Her dismissive laugh did something to him, and he pulled her flush against him. Her aloof demeanor changed to one of surprise…and awareness. Colin's lips curled in triumph. Her voice was a husky whisper when she said, "This is not exactly how I usually conduct business."

His shoulders tensed at the thought of her dancing with other men, looking the way she did tonight. He blew out a breath through his nose and deliberately drew his shoulder back down. It was none of his god-damn business whom she danced with.

"Like I said, sometimes impulsivity leads to the best sort of fun." Taking on a life of its own, his thumb drew soft circles on her lower back. "How else would we have had this great opportunity to build rapport?"

"Now it's rapport-building?" She held his eyes and her lips lifted into a *Mona Lisa* smile. "This keeps getting better and better."

With their heads bent close to hear each other, the sexy-as-hell hint of whiskey on her breath was driving him wild. He lowered his head imperceptibly to breathe in her scent, and she shivered in his arms. She felt the magnetic pull, too, and it was damn hot. When her eyes searched his, he slowly angled his head until their lips were mere inches apart.

Both of them drew back as though lightning had struck them. They were dancing in the middle of a crowd. They couldn't do this. Breathing roughly, they gazed at each other in wonder and panic, not quite knowing what to do next. Then a look of stubborn determination filled her face, and Jihae slowly rose to her toes, shocking the hell out of him. She was so bold and true to her feelings. He respected her and wanted her exponentially more. And he wanted to kiss her full, red lips. So badly.

But he jerked himself back at the last second and eased her into a spin. When they faced each other again, he held himself stiffly apart from her. No matter what happened, he wouldn't seduce her. What had compelled him to nearly kiss her had nothing to do with his plans to earn her trust, but the end result would be the same. He couldn't use her that way.

"Yes, rapport-building," he continued as though there hadn't been a sizable lapse in their conversation. "This is definitely more effective than a company retreat."

"I trust you're as discreet as you are professional." Her determined expression was replaced by a hint of mortification. *Damn it.* He hated making her feel rejected, but it was the honorable thing to do. "Jumping around and dancing like a crazy woman doesn't meld with my business image. Neither does dancing in the arms of my partner. I don't intend to repeat either of these activities."

"I'm not the gossiping sort if that's what you're asking," he said, hoping to ease her concern. "But this is hardly a matter that requires discretion. We're two adults sharing a dance. Not exactly top gossip material. Besides, I don't think anyone here recognizes you, and my presence here is expected."

"So you're a regular here?" She leaned back in his arms to look at him. "Should I assume you're something of a party animal by night and a businessman by day?"

"I'm a businessman day and night." He allowed himself a small smile, anticipating her surprise. "I own Pendulum."

She didn't disappoint. She gasped sharply, her eyes becoming wide saucers. Nightclub Jihae was the perfect amalgam of sexy and adorable. "What do you mean you own Pendulum? Wait, forget I just said that. That was a silly question. Of course I understand what you're saying."

"You're right to be surprised. Not everyone runs nightclubs on the side while growing a production company. It's not a well-known fact, especially in the film industry. I'm just known as the new kid on the block."

"Did you say 'nightclubs'?"

"Yes, I own three others, but I started with Pendulum." To his regret, the song came to an end, and he let his arms drop to his sides, sadly bereft of her warmth. "She's something special."

"Well, then." Curiosity saturated her face, as they arrived at her table to find June's rapt attention on them. "It was nice running in to you, Colin."

"Yes. It was very nice," he said, extending his hand to her. The jolt of electricity made his body hum again. His body was even more aware of her after having held her in his arms. He quickly withdrew his hand, breaking contact. He had to walk away this minute because he was barely holding it together. "Good seeing you, June."

"Mmm-hmm." June didn't exactly roll her eyes, but he sensed her attitude nonetheless. He must have looked like an eager pup, panting after Jihae. He had to stop being so obvious, so he furrowed his brow to look more serious. Because, well, he was an idiot. He probably looked like a ridiculous caricature.

"Well, then. I hope you ladies enjoy the rest of the night, and your drinks are on the house."

"You don't need to—"

"Thank you, Colin," June said cheerily, cutting off her friend's protest.

He smiled his approval at her, then inclined his head to both of them. "Good night."

Jihae bit her bottom lip as though she wanted to say something but simply said, "Good night."

Colin sighed in relief. He didn't think he could handle her company much longer without doing things that could jeopardize their partnership as well as his personal objective. The woman was sinfully alluring and he was no saint.

He went back to the bar, walked behind it and grabbed himself a half-empty bottle of cognac and a glass. Tim acknowledged Colin's little indulgence with a wave of his hand and shooed him out of his space. After throwing a smirk over his shoulder, Colin went inside his office and closed the door.

He intended to drown his lust in liquor so it wouldn't be able to resurface too soon. Yes, it would resurface. Colin was never one to deny the inevitable. He just wanted to delay it.

Six

She was fully encased in her Princess Jihae armor as she waited for her elevator. She needed it more than ever as she headed to her meeting with Colin. It'd been a couple of weeks since they'd run in to each other at Pendulum, but she still felt raw and exposed when she thought of how she'd behaved.

Jihae had no excuse or explanation for her impulsive actions that night. She'd just done what she wanted to for once. She hadn't cared about anything but being in his arms. Being pressed against him. And wanting to kiss him.

Remembering how Colin pulled away from her made her blush with mortification, but she also felt another, more troublesome emotion. Regret. Despite everything, she wished she'd kissed the hell out of him, and the ferocity of her desire scared her. She'd had a couple of discreet affairs before, but she had never felt the thrill she experienced with Colin.

Did she regret the partnership with CS Productions? No. The project was proceeding like a dream and her excitement grew every day. It was worth the physical and mental toll of denying her attraction to Colin. He'd asked her to come to his office, which probably meant he had a presentation ready for her. She was looking forward to the meeting.

But it would be a shame to be indoors on such a beautiful day. And…that was the strangest thought. When had she ever spent a workday enjoying the outdoors and the sun? The answer was never. Unless she was scouting a location, but she would be too focused on what she was doing to appreciate the experience. *Wonky.* She gave herself a mental shake.

After tasting a bit of fun, she craved it like an addiction. Well, enough of that. Today was going to be a day of air-conditioned offices, dimmed lights and PowerPoint presentations. But she was still excited to find out about prospective directors. She had a few ideas of her own, but Colin had the insider knowledge.

As she drove toward his office, she decided now was a great time to enjoy some sun and rolled down her top, uncaring about what the wind would to do her low chignon. Maybe she could wear her hair down today. Go bonkers. She laughed and let the breeze carry it away. What kind of life was she living when she couldn't even choose her own hairstyle? But the sun was warm on her neck and arms, and the breeze was cool without being too cold. She didn't feel like she was a prisoner in her own life at the moment. She felt free and vibrant.

Jihae briefly regretted her impulsivity when she parked at Colin's office and checked her appearance in the rearview mirror. She had loose strands of hair framing her face and falling down her back, and her cheeks were as red as spring blossoms. Her princess armor had gone askew. She gave up trying to fix her hair and got out of her car. No one was going to notice a bit of windblown hair.

When she walked into the office, she was immediately greeted by an eager, fresh-faced young man. "Hello, Ms. Park. I'm Ethan. It's a pleasure to finally meet you. And this is my colleague Kimberly."

"It's nice to meet you," Kimberly said.

"I'm so glad to meet CS Productions's team members. I think we're going to have an amazing time working on this film together," Jihae said, shaking their hands.

She was subtly scanning the open-plan work space and wondering where Colin could be when he strolled out of his office with a messenger bag strapped across his shoulders. He was in a casual button-down shirt, rolled up to his elbows, and a pair of khakis. He looked tanned and athletic. She, in her usual white dress suit and python heels, probably looked boring and anemic beside him.

"Come on, Jihae," he said, leading her to the exit by a gentle hold on her elbow. "We have to go."

"Where are we going?" she asked, waving hastily at Ethan and Kimberly. "I thought we were having a discussion about the potential directors."

"We are," he said, not bothering to elaborate. He was up to something, and she was dying to find out what it was.

She lengthened her strides to keep up with Colin as they left the office "Then where are we going?"

"To the zoo."

"The zoo?" She skidded to a halt, a few feet from what she assumed was his car. "Whatever for?"

"I think better when I'm walking, and the zoo is a great place to walk. It's never too crowded on weekdays and it's quiet."

Jihae's heart flipped. Another adventure. She glanced at the easy grin on Colin's face and felt her heart melt a little. Doing business didn't mean you couldn't have fun. She appreciated and admired his way of thinking and his easygoing manner. She could get used to working with him in this new way. Much too easily, in fact.

"Well, what if the lions roar and drown out our conversation?" she joked, her heart beating faster.

"Nah. California lions are way too chill to roar." He walked a few steps to his car and held open the passenger door. "Besides, they're too cool for school, so they stay inside their caves most of the time."

She sat down and buckled her seat belt, and bounced the tiniest bit in her seat. She had actually been to a zoo in Korea when she was a child, but it was before the zoo was open to the public. It was just her, the zoo administrator and her tutor in the spacious animal park. The grounds had been shadowed in the early morning light, and the animals had seemed too sleepy to play.

Visiting a zoo in daylight with Colin by her side filled her with giddy anticipation. But, of course, this was still a business meeting and they had work to get done. She shouldn't forget that or think that he was doing this for her benefit in any way.

"So how often do you go to the zoo to work?" she asked.

Colin shifted in his seat and coughed into his fist. "Not often enough."

Hmm. Was he embarrassed about being a regular at the zoo? "Where else do you go to think?"

"Um…the museum," he blurted. "The museum is another great place to walk and think."

Jihae absolutely loved museums but she hadn't had an opportunity to visit the ones in Los Angeles yet. "Oh, that sounds lovely. I've been wanting to go to LACMA and the Getty Center."

"We could have our next meeting at the Getty Center."

She nearly clapped her hands and cheered. But she held herself in check. "Perhaps."

He shot a glance at her and smirked like he could see right through her. She turned up her nose at him and held her answering smile in check. They drove the rest of the way in comfortable silence with random observations here and there, but anticipation wound up her stomach.

The zoo looked like a wonderland in the glorious California sunshine, and Jihae felt her spirits rise even higher.

"Ticket for two adults, please," said Colin, reaching for his wallet in his back pocket.

God, how do you get an ass that perfect? Before she got too entranced by his backside, Jihae spoke up. "Hey, you don't have to wine and dine me anymore. We're partners. I'll pay for this."

"But it was my idea…"

"And it'll be my treat," she replied, handing over her card.

Colin grumbled under his breath but didn't protest any further. His mood lifted as soon as they walked into the park to be greeted by neon pink flamingos.

"They smell horrible but they are such a lively sight," he said in a nasally voice. He was breathing through his mouth, as she was.

"I agree to both observations."

"Let's find an animal we could breathe better around, and we could chat about some of the ideas my team and I came up with."

Jihae's shoulders drooped a little at the mention of business. Just for a moment, she'd imagined them to be simply enjoying each other's company. Such silliness. "Good idea. I have some ideas of my own."

The next animals they visited were the giraffes. They were quiet and still except for munching leaves in their mouths. Their heads were so high up, she didn't have to worry about them eavesdropping on their production plans.

"Kimberly did a very thorough job of research-ing and weighing the pros and cons of each of the directors she selected for my preliminary review. I've chosen five of them for you to consider. I have my favorite but I won't tell you until you share your thoughts."

"Who are they?"

"Stella Merles, Edward Stein, Ken Park, Cora Huang and Mateo Sanchez." Colin counted off his fingers.

"Mateo Sanchez?"

"Yup."

"He's done some amazing work," she said, excited to have a director of his caliber on their list. "I think he would be sensitive to how we want to treat diver-sity."

"But Cora Huang did an incredible job with her last two films," he said, pushing back from the rail-ing and motioning for her to walk with him. "I was blown away by how she portrayed the female protag-onists to be both strong and vulnerable, and to grow with all the clumsiness and faltering of real people."

"All your picks have their own special strengths. I could narrow it down to three at best, but from there on, I wouldn't know who to pick. I would be thrilled to have any of them."

Colin chuckled and said, "You know, the choice isn't entirely up to us. Those directors are hot com-modities. They may turn us down."

Jihae lifted her chin and gave him her haughtiest

look. "If I set my mind on something, I don't take no for an answer."

It was true. She was relentless. Of course, she didn't always get what she wanted, but it wasn't for not giving it her everything. Some things were worth fighting for.

Colin was quiet for a while as he led them to their next animal. She glanced around and took in her surroundings, and sighed a little wistfully. She couldn't deny that she enjoyed these easy moments with him.

He stopped in front of the elephants and rested his hand on the railing. When Jihae stopped beside him and saw the baby elephant standing by its mama, she couldn't hold back her *aww*. Colin turned and awarded her with a wide grin, and she smiled back happily. The mama and baby elephants were the cutest sight. She stepped closer to the railing and held on with her hands, wanting to be near them.

She inadvertently brushed her pinkie against his, and pulled back as a tremor traveled down her back. She glanced at him from under her lashes, pretending to watch the elephants. Her hand looked pale and small next to his darker, bigger one. An image of their intertwined fingers seared itself into her mind, and she wanted it to be real. She could almost feel the warmth of his hand and the heat burning through her veins.

As though reading her mind, Colin placed his hand over hers and laced their fingers together. Neither of them said anything. They both looked down at their entangled hands with quickening breaths. Finally, his eyes, full of gentle yearning, sought hers out, and she fell into their depths.

"Come with me?" he asked with a soft squeeze of her hand.

"Yes."

His steps weren't hurried as he led them down the miniature streets of the zoo. But he picked up speed when they arrived at the entrance of a small aquarium. A narrow, dark hallway led them inside and continued into a semicircle as it opened up into a round aquarium that hugged the outer walls. The blue light emanating from the water gave the interior an otherworldly vibe. And it was deserted.

Colin didn't stop until they walked into another dark hallway leading into what she presumed was another exhibition. He maneuvered her back against the wall and ran his hands up and down her arms, making her shiver with anticipation.

"I shouldn't do this," he said in a rough, low voice.

"Neither should I." She wrapped her arms around his neck. "Kiss me?"

"God, yes," he said, crushing his mouth against hers.

Jihae let herself melt against him with a content sigh. When his tongue gently outlined her bottom lip, she parted her mouth and flicked her tongue against his. That earned her a sexy growl from Colin, and his hands pressed against her back, bringing her even closer to him.

Her curious hands traveled down the length of his firm, muscular arms and came to rest on his narrow waist. First her thumbs drew circles on his stomach, then she boldly grabbed his shirt and tugged it out of his pants. She didn't stop there. She couldn't. She wanted to touch him. To feel him.

He hummed under his breath and pressed his torso into her hands, so she followed her instincts without hesitation. Her fingers traveled over his stomach, delighting in every muscled groove. Then she moved her palms onto his hard, broad chest. It was so smooth. So hot.

Meanwhile, he kissed her like a man starved, but kept his hands planted firmly on her back. He was holding himself in check—trembling beneath her hands—to give her control of how far they would go. They were semihidden in the darkness of the hallway, but they didn't exactly have privacy. This shouldn't go far at all, but she wanted it to last just a little bit longer.

"Goddammit." Colin suddenly pulled back to her bewilderment. "Sorry. It's not the kiss. It's not you. I just have a call I need to return."

Then in the recesses of her mind, Jihae recalled the subtle ringing of a gong. It must have come from Colin's phone. He walked through to the other side, his phone against his ear. She stayed behind to give him privacy and to take a moment to gather herself. She realized she was shaking, as well, and she breathed deeply in and out. After straightening her suit, she finally followed Colin into the next room.

The lights were even dimmer in this section, shining purple, blue and pink to exhibit the multicolored, glowing jellyfish that filled the various tanks. The firm line of Colin's lips and the frown creasing his forehead looked out of place in the beautiful setting. Soon he ended his call and turned to her, his expression transforming into a regretful smile.

"I'm sorry. I'm afraid we need to leave," he said.

"Leave?"

"I'll drive you back to your car."

"My car?" She knew she was repeating everything he said, but she didn't understand. They'd just shared a passionate kiss, and he was going to dump her at her car. Shouldn't they go someplace to talk? Or kiss some more?

"I'm so sorry," he said again. "We'll talk later."

His grandmother had uncanny timing.

He was beyond frustrated by her interruption, and…grateful. He'd lost his head. No, he'd known exactly what he was doing, and he hadn't wanted to stop. Jihae had tasted improbably like a summer day—like the warm sun and a soft breeze. Then she'd sucked him in like a sultry, tropical night. Her soft, cool hands exploring his body, and her sweet, wet lips kissing him with a hunger to match his own. No, he'd never wanted to stop.

But Grandmother's call had been like a bucket of ice-cold water thrown at his face. A much-needed wake-up call. He couldn't kiss Jihae forever. He shouldn't have kissed her in the first place. Not only were they business partners, but he was also a Song. His cousin had broken their engagement, and she had sought revenge against him. They had quite a sordid backstory, except Jihae didn't know yet. What was worse was that he planned to spy on her. He couldn't risk having her become emotionally attached to him. He had no intention of breaking her heart. Ever.

Their drive back to his office had been tense and silent. Was it regret that had clouded her expression? His gut clenched. *Hell.* He couldn't believe that he felt disappointed at the thought. Was he kidding himself that the kiss was a mistake that he never intended to repeat?

Before he could dissect his jumbled thoughts, he arrived at his grandmother's Pacific Palisades home. He parked in the driveway and jumped out of the car. He was glad he could escape his confused emotions. And he had other things to worry about. He was quite positive that his grandmother had found out about CS Productions's partnership with Rotelle Entertainment.

"Hello, beautiful," he said when Liliana, the Song family's housekeeper, opened the door.

"Hello, handsome boy," Liliana said, laughing, and tousled his hair. "Mrs. Song is in her study. What trouble have you gotten yourself into today?"

His mind immediately flashed back to the darkened halls of the aquarium with Jihae sighing and arching into his body. He shook his head and flashed Liliana his daredevil smile. "What have I *not* gotten myself into is the question."

Despite his flippant words, he walked down the hall with solemn steps. He thought he'd prepared himself for this, but one could never be fully prepared to face off with Grace Song. After taking a deep breath, he knocked on the study door.

"Come in," she ordered.

He opened the door then closed it behind him. Despite his instinct to hightail it out of there, Colin walked up to his grandmother and bowed. "Hal-muh-nee, have you been well?"

"I had been rather well, but I'm not so sure at the moment," she said with a slight downward turn of her mouth. "Are you ready to explain yourself?"

Damn. She was pissed off. She usually began her interrogations with complete stoicism. The tension in the corners of her mouth didn't bode well for him. Was he ready to explain himself? *No.* "Yes."

"What in the world prompted you to partner with Jihae Park? After what she and her family tried to do?"

"Jihae Park and I aren't partners. I don't seem to have the romantic luck that Garrett and Adelaide have," he quipped, but quickly turned down the humor when his grandmother's eyes narrowed with impatience. "CS Productions entered into a promising partnership with Rotelle Entertainment. It has nothing to do with us personally."

"And who might this *us* be?"

"Jihae and me."

"*Jihae* and you are an *us* to you?"

An emotion between fear and doubt churned through him. "Grandmother, you're playing word games with me. If you think I've forgotten what Rotelle tried to do to Garrett, then you don't know me at all. I'm not only looking out for CS Productions's interests but those of our family."

"You're not altogether wrong about me being a little unreasonable right now," she conceded with a sigh. "But we almost lost Natalie and the baby because of the Parks. Well, them, and Garrett behaving like a complete fool by pushing Natalie away like that. All in all, it's not something I could easily forget or forgive."

"And that brings me to my second motivation for entering into a partnership with Rotelle Entertainment." Colin sat forward in his seat. "Jihae Park doesn't know that I'm your grandson, since we've made sure that only our family and our oldest friends know."

"Go on."

"I could earn her trust and find evidence of Rotelle Corporation's involvement in the espionage attempt against Hansol."

"While you work with her on a project that will benefit CS Productions? Do you think that wise? Or honorable?"

"Honorable? They're the ones who started the war. I only mean to end it with justice."

"Technically, Garrett began the war by refusing her hand. I have to take partial responsibility for that, as well."

"Are you defending them now?" Colin couldn't understand his grandmother's reaction. Didn't she want the Parks brought to justice?

"Not at all. The only one I care about in this

twisted farce is you, my child." Grandmother sighed, shaking her head slowly. "You've told me, and shown me, how much CS Productions means to you. You are putting your company at risk by this stunt you're intending to pull. What happens to the partnership if she finds out who you are? What happens when she finds out you've set out to betray her and her family from the start?"

"Jihae is a brilliant businesswoman. I don't believe she would jeopardize the film because of a personal falling-out. She wouldn't. I know her." But Colin also knew that Jihae would never forgive him for intending to spy on her.

"Suk-ah," his grandmother said, her tone softening with the use of his Korean name. "Listen to yourself. You believe Jihae Park to possess integrity. If what you say of her is true, then I find it hard to believe that she was involved in the corporate espionage. Perhaps she's in the dark about what Rotelle Corporation did. Or perhaps your objectivity has already been compromised. Either way, if you keep pushing yourself to spy on Rotelle Corporation through her, I'm afraid you'll only be harming CS Productions and your conscience."

Colin realized that she was right. The more time he spent with Jihae, the harder it was to believe that she was involved in her family's attempt to sabotage the Hansol-Vivotex partnership, not to mention Garrett's marriage. What he knew of Jihae did not fit such subterfuge. But maybe he was allowing his attraction to her cloud his judgment. He refused to let that happen.

"I apologize for not agreeing with you, Hal-muh-nee. The partnership with Rotelle Entertainment will put CS Productions on the map, and working closely with Jihae will allow me to bring Rotelle Corporation to justice."

"Rotelle *and* Jihae, you mean?"

"Yes," he said through clenched teeth.

"Rotelle Corporation should pay for their crime, but I don't want this bad blood to affect your future. The espionage attempt was ultimately a failure, and Garrett and Natalie are happy as can be," Grandmother said, searching his face. "I understand and accept your professional judgment in forming a partnership with Rotelle Entertainment, but compromising your integrity to bring someone else to justice could bring you down to their level in a blink of an eye."

"If you're worried about me losing my way, please don't. I know exactly what I'm doing." *Ha.* He was so conflicted and lost. He needed his grandmother's guidance more than ever.

"You have always been the most stubborn child," she huffed. "Despite what you believe, I am happy that you are doing so well on your own. It is true I would be happier if you were thriving in Hansol, but you did not disappoint me. There is nothing to make amends for or repay. We are family, and I am your grandmother. Do not let a false sense of gratitude or guilt persuade you to harm your conscience or integrity."

"Thank you for your reassurance, Hal-muh-nee."

A suffocating weight lifted off his chest at his grandmother's words. He had no idea how much he needed
to hear that. "And I will take your advice to heart."

Grandmother was right. He wasn't convinced of
Jihae's guilt as he had first been, and the thought of
actively gaining her trust just to betray her made him
sick to his stomach. Besides, he wasn't getting anywhere with it. He hadn't even been able to take the
few opportunities he had to steal a glimpse at Jihae's
computer because his conscience got in the way.

He would continue to be alert and on the look-
out for information about Rotelle Corporation, but he
would focus on producing the best film he could and
take a step back from the amateur sleuth business.

Seven

Well, two could play at this game. If Colin wanted to pretend that nothing happened between them, then she would happily oblige. *Maybe not happily, but still.* Her willpower had proven to be shamefully weak when it came to Colin Song. It wasn't that she had forgotten why she couldn't be with him, but when she was with him, it all seemed so distant and…trivial.

What harm could a brief fling do? She knew how to be discreet in her affairs. No one had to find out. Then what was holding her back? *You're afraid of wanting more. That's what.* Colin Song's pull on her was something she'd never felt with anyone else. And the spirit she'd hidden deep inside her to appease her parents flared back to life in response. Wanting him, having him, could mean the unraveling of the precarious balance she had forced on her life.

And she didn't think she wanted to lose that balance. She was…content with the little bit of freedom she found in the United States, and working on *Best Placed Bets* was a longtime dream finally coming true. She just needed to get lost in her work. That was her safe place. She was confident when she worked and was damn good at what she did. She never had to doubt or second-guess her business instincts. Jihae could not let a man make her falter.

She had been summoned to do her father's bidding—through the impersonal email of his executive assistant—for yet another affiliate. The brain-numbing job of smiling and reassuring Rotelle Chemical that Chairman Park was pleased with their work and dining on tiny, expensive meals should keep her busy for the day. Then it was on to two other facilities for the opening of their factories. Spending a week away from LA, and Colin, would do her good. It would slow down her libido from hyperdrive. And when she returned, she would focus 100 percent on her job.

Jihae returned to LA after a week away, but focusing 100 percent on her job was turning out to be a pipe dream. She'd missed the darn man during her entire trip, and now that she was back, their kiss refused to leave her head.

"You're doing it again," June said, barely glancing up from the TV.

It was their weekly movie-bingeing night. It really

was part of Jihae's job, but watching the movies with June made it a lot more fun. But then again, her best friend was being massively irritating at the moment.

"No, I'm not," Jihae insisted, making sure she wasn't wearing the slightest smile or frown on her face. In other words, she slid on her Princess Jihae face.

"Remember, your ice-princess mask doesn't work on me, dummy."

"Will you just stop it?" She took a huge bite of her pizza.

"I'm just saying." June shrugged and munched on her own slice. "That kiss wasn't just a lapse in good judgment, like you insist. You get that sparkling Disney princess face every time you daydream about it. Then, you turn all red and blotchy, and get psychopath-eyed."

"Shut up. Please." It was true, so Jihae didn't want to hear it.

"He still hasn't called you?"

"No," she said, sliding her plate away from her. Her ravenous appetite had vanished like magic. Instead, she reached for her red wine and took a healthy gulp. "Kimberly is lining up the interviews. She's been keeping you posted, right?"

"Right. So you're avoiding direct contact with him, as well?" June rolled her eyes. "You guys are so juvenile."

The week spent away from LA and Rotelle Entertainment, and pretending that nothing had happened between her and Colin, had not made Jihae forget the kiss they'd shared in the dark, glowing hallways of the aquarium. His taste, his warmth, his smell. Her body heated up by several degrees every time she remembered their kiss. It wasn't just the physical pleasure of the encounter, but the connection she'd felt with him. He'd made her feel safe and cherished, like she'd never felt before. And more than anything, she wanted to feel that again despite all logic dictating against a repeat of their kiss.

But then, he'd just up and left. Acted as though nothing had happened between them. And as June pointed out, he hadn't said a word to her since he'd dropped her off at her car that day. She felt bewildered and indignant...and she just wanted to hear his voice. So much.

This foreign need inside her to yearn so desperately for someone both frightened her and made her feel more alive. When it came to business, she never hesitated to reach for what she wanted. Why did this have to be any different? Certainly, there were risks and obstacles, but weren't risks and obstacles present in everything worth having in life?

She tried to convince herself that it was her lady parts doing the thinking. That if she'd wanted a chance to be with Colin Song, she shouldn't have partnered Rotelle Entertainment with CS Productions. But it was no good. She wanted the partnership *and* Colin.

It was a relief to finally admit to herself that she wanted Colin Song. And she was going to win him over. No man had ever made her feel the way he did, and maybe no other man ever would. She needed to take this chance to explore her attraction to him.

But would a personal relationship with him impact their working relationship? She and Colin were mature adults and professionals. They would be able to keep their personal life separate from their work. Besides, how different could it be from their current situation? She already thought of him constantly and discreetly ogled him when he was around. She just had to remember not to make her infatuation obvious to everyone around them.

She was a smart woman. She knew how to be careful and neutralize risks. Even her father had never found out about her other lovers. Well, there were only two of them, but she had chosen men who hadn't come from money, men her father wouldn't have approved of. Men she respected. If her father had known, he wouldn't have looked the other way. There was no reason she couldn't keep her personal interactions with Colin a secret. *But what if you want something lasting with him? Something real?*

The thought came unbidden, and she had no answers. As far as she knew, he didn't come from a well-known, wealthy family. Her father would frown on such "lack of pedigree." Was she willing to oppose her father to be with a man her family wouldn't accept? Would she be willing to give up Rotelle Entertainment for Colin? *Never mind all that.* She would cross that road if she ever got to it.

"I wasn't allowed to be juvenile even when I was a child. I'm not going to start acting like a child as a grown woman," Jihae announced to a startled June, who thought she'd had the last word.

"Okay, then. Are you going to call him?"

"Nope."

"For God's sake—"

Jihae cut her off before she could resume her nagging. "I'm going to see him in person."

"Right on," June said, raising her palm in the air.

She high-fived her friend and stood up. "Right now."

Her decision made, Jihae felt bold and determined. She rushed to the parking structure and pulled out onto the street before voice-dialing Colin.

"Hello, Jihae." He picked up the phone just as she was about to hang up, and his tone was oh-so-casual.

"Hi." Had he been busy or was he contemplating not answering her call? "Are you working late tonight?"

"Yes, but not for CS Productions. I'm catching up on business at Pendulum."

Bingo. "Were you able to make things official with Charity Banning?"

"I was planning to email you about that tomorrow. We reached an oral agreement, and Ethan will be communicating with June to draw up a formal contract."

"Excellent news. I'm glad I got to hear it tonight."

There was slight hesitation on his end. "Is that why you called?"

"That was part of it."

"And the other part?" he asked in a low, coaxing voice.

Was he flirting with her? If he was going to be like this, why hadn't he just called? He was the one who had rudely cut short their kissing session. Her indignation suddenly rose again. She wasn't going to make this easy for him.

"I actually can't recall the other part. It must not have been very important," she said archly. "Good night, Colin. Congratulations on Charity Banning."

"But—"

She hung up, cutting off his protest. *That felt good.* Hanging up on him gave her some immature satisfaction. Now she was going to invade his home turf and show him exactly what the other part was about.

Traffic was moderate and she made good time to Pendulum. She checked her reflection in the rearview mirror. Her eyes were bright and her color heightened. Adrenaline. Pure, natural makeup. She was wearing a white sleeveless mock neck and a pair of wide-legged white slacks. She wasn't exactly dressed for a nightclub, but she wore her hair down and a swipe of clear lip gloss made her adequately presentable.

Jihae got past the bouncers without a hitch and approached the host. "Hi, I'm here to see Mr. Song."

"Is he expecting you, miss?" the gentleman asked, giving her a perfunctory once-over. She seemed to meet his approval.

"We spoke on the phone only a few minutes ago."

"Then let me escort you to his office."

"I don't want to disrupt your duties. Pointing me in the right direction is all I need."

"Very well. Go down that hallway and turn left. You'll see one door marked *Employees Only* and an unmarked door across from it. That's his office."

"Thank you so much, Mr...."

"Tucker. Just Tucker is fine," he said with a smile.

"Thank you, Tucker. I'm Jihae."

"Nice to meet you, Jihae."

With a wave, she strode toward Colin's office. But once she got there, her nerves faltered for a moment. Then, with an impatient shake of her head, she knocked smartly on the door.

"Come in."

His voice was clear but he sounded a bit distracted. He was probably immersed in his work. But when she stepped inside, he was staring down at his phone, his thumbs at rest.

"I remembered the other reason I called," she said softly.

Colin's head shot up and the intensity of his gaze stole her breath. He pushed back from his desk, making his chair spin wildly, and took three long strides to come stand in front of her. Her heart pounded bruisingly against her ribs, and all her confident resolve seemed to melt.

"Care to share what it is?" he said in a low growl.

She swallowed and gathered her wits about her. "Your urgent business at the zoo that day? Were you able to take care of it satisfactorily?"

"Satisfactorily? No. Far from it," he said, his eyes

dropping to her lips. "All I managed to do was feed the fire."

"Kiss me." Her breaths came in short puffs.

"No."

"No?" Her shock overshadowed her hurt at his rejection. He was trembling in front of her, his eyes near manic. He wanted her as much as she wanted him. "Why ever not?"

"We work together. You have built up this image of yourself as the untouchable ice queen. If word gets out that we've slept together, it could taint your image. This industry is brutal. They would use any weakness to undermine you."

"Who said anything about sleeping together?" Jihae said with exaggerated surprise. "I thought we could make out a few more times, and maybe have some oral fun. You're getting way ahead of yourself."

Colin looked at her like he wanted to rip off her clothes and take her against the wall twice. Jihae sucked in a quick breath and continued, "Besides, there's no reason anyone needs to know. We're both intelligent adults. I'm sure the two of us will find a way to keep whatever we do completely discreet."

"Don't do this," he said, his eyes pleading. He was almost hers. "You don't know what you're getting yourself into."

"I always know what I'm getting myself into." She closed the distance between them and tugged him roughly by his collar. "And just to make myself clear, I'm doing this. Very thoroughly."

She crushed her lips against him and moaned in

relief when Colin met her lips with possessive heat. She'd been dreaming of kissing him again and she wasn't going to waste any time. She parted her lips and slid her tongue against his bottom lip, then lightly bit it.

"God," he moaned.

When he opened up as she'd wanted, Jihae took full advantage of the situation and plunged her tongue inside the warmth of his mouth. He groaned deep in his throat and the last of his reserve seemed to shatter. He spread his hands wide against her back and brought her flush against his body. Then he overtook the languid sweeping of her tongue and plunged his into her mouth again and again.

She whimpered and pressed her hips into him, needing to be closer, and felt his hard length dig into her pelvis. Satisfaction flooded her and she was gripped by power. With fumbling hands, Jihae pulled his shirt out of his slacks then smoothed her palms over the firm ridges of his stomach and slid them up to his broad chest. He jerked beneath her hands and ground his hips into her. She couldn't help it. A low, sultry laugh escaped from her lips. She was high on the power she held over him.

"You like that, do you?" His voice held a hint of danger, and a thrill ran down her spine.

"Oh, yes. Very much."

He groaned in answer and spun her to press her back against a wall. His hands slipped to her bottom and squeezed, and her eyes nearly rolled back in her head.

"Colin."

"Jihae. You're so beautiful."

He hiked her leg around his waist, and rocked his hips against her center, making her moan low and long. Colin clapped a hand over her mouth, and kissed a trail of fire down the side of her neck. The hand that had been holding her hip released its hold, and came to rest right below her breast. His thumb moved slowly back and forth on the bottom curve and she arched her back, giving him permission to explore farther.

"Shh," he warned before removing his hand from her mouth.

Returning his left hand to tightly secure her leg around his waist, he worked his right hand under her top. He smoothed his hand across her stomach, reclaimed her lips and murmured words of sweet adoration against them. With excruciating gentleness, he slid his hand up, cupped her breast and twirled his thumb over the lace of her bra.

She wiggled against him and pushed into his hand. With a sexy, arrogant laugh, he bent his head and licked the mound above the bra like it was the most decadent scoop of ice cream. She shivered against him with a lusty sigh as he continued to torture her. Unable to handle any more, she reached to tug down her bra and thrust her peak against his lips.

With a guttural groan, Colin succumbed to her will and tasted her nipple, twirling his tongue around it and pulling it deeply into his mouth.

"Colin," she whimpered as her frantic hands reached for his belt. She needed him inside her. Now.

Colin was so turned on he could hardly see straight. Her creamy, pink-tipped breasts tasted as sweet as honey, and her skin slid beneath his hands like warm silk. He was so hard that it almost hurt, and when she cried out his name, he thought he was going to lose it in his pants.

He was so lost in her that it didn't register in his brain what her hands were doing. When she freed his belt and unbuttoned the top of his pants, he finally understood. For a split second, he wanted to succumb to her siren's call. He was dying to feel her soft, warm hand on his aching dick. Then he remembered why he shouldn't kiss her, much less make love to her.

"Don't," he ordered in a ragged voice, grasping her wrists to stop her from going any farther. She stilled at his command, her whole body going stiff against his. He mourned the loss of the languid warmth of her aroused body. But no. He couldn't do this. He shouldn't. "We need to stop."

Slowly, he righted her bra and tugged down her shirt to cover her glorious bare skin. Then he stepped back, tucked his shirt into his slacks and buckled his belt. He couldn't meet Jihae's eyes. He hadn't meant for things to go so far, but when she'd walked into his office, he knew he was going to kiss her. Her boldness and sweet vulnerability were his undoing. But now, he'd pushed her away, and the last thing he wanted to do was hurt her.

He finally looked up to find her staring right at him. He wasn't sure what he'd expected to find—maybe embarrassment and regret—but it certainly wasn't cold fury.

"That's it?" she asked. "Are you going to avoid me for months now? Are you going to pretend this never happened, too?"

"Jihae, that's not—"

"I am not a fragile porcelain doll that you need to protect. Even if I were fragile—and I certainly am not—it isn't your job to protect me. I can take care of myself. If you offer me your bullshit about protecting my reputation again, I will kick your skittish ass."

"It's not that simple—"

She cut him off again. "This is the last time I offer myself to you. You want me, but you're too afraid to take a chance. Well, listen very carefully. I will have you on your knees before I ever let you lay a finger on me again. On. Your. Knees."

That was the sexiest angry speech he had ever heard. He definitely felt like he'd been put in his place, but it was so incredibly hot. Since thinking of pleasurable ways to get on his knees for her wasn't conducive to getting his body under control, and Jihae needed to leave his office before he lost all willpower, he decided to just keep his mouth shut. He couldn't think of what to say at any rate. Other than *wow*.

She arched a perfect eyebrow when he didn't offer any more excuses, then tsked impatiently. "I'll see you next week for the director interviews. Good night."

With that, she opened the door and walked out

of his office with her head held high. Colin was relieved that their last two kissing sessions weren't going to affect their business relationship. He wasn't surprised, though. Jihae was a true professional and she wouldn't let her personal life interfere with her work. If he'd liked and respected her before tonight, he was in awe of her now. She was spectacular in every way.

He'd been doubting his initial belief that Jihae had been involved in Rotelle's espionage scheme. After tonight, he couldn't believe that she'd been a part of it. Despite her impenetrable ice-queen image, Jihae was frank, honest and fair, and was an incredible partner to work with. She had such innate integrity that she gave praise and credit where it was due, and wasn't afraid to admit when she was wrong.

Could such a person have participated in such subterfuge? Colin's gut instinct told him no. And he would never hold her accountable for the depravities of her family. Rotelle was still the prime suspect for the espionage attack against Hansol, but he wouldn't wrap Jihae into it anymore. Maybe he could even trust her enough to ask her outright if she knew anything about the espionage. No, that would be crazy. He couldn't do that without revealing his connection to the Song family. While she didn't allow her personal life to interfere with her work, working with her ex-fiancé's cousin would probably be too much, even for her. And, more importantly, Jihae wouldn't betray her family.

Despite the guilt nagging insistently at him, he had

to keep his identity a secret for the sake of the production. He didn't want to be a constant reminder of her broken engagement and her injured pride. Jihae was as invested as he was in the project. He couldn't ruin things for her by putting her in such an impossible position.

Colin swiped his hands down his face. Preparations for the production were going into overdrive soon, and he would have to spend a lot of time with Jihae. Hopefully, she didn't hate his guts after tonight, and they could go back to being good colleagues.

The thought of being "good colleagues" with the most alluring woman he had the pleasure of meeting plunged him into a black mood. A platonic relationship with Jihae was as appealing as climbing a rocky mountain with bare feet. The lust blazing inside him was likely to burn him to cinders, but he had no other choice.

He had to protect Jihae from himself, find justice for his family and make a damn good movie.

Eight

Jihae was a strong-willed woman. She didn't regret throwing herself at him, but she was most definitely not going to give in again. She'd meant every word she said. He would need to beg to have her after that spectacular rejection. She'd spent a lifetime playing the role of Princess Jihae. While it took monumental willpower not to touch him, she was able to exude cool professionalism on the outside.

With the director and screenwriter selected, they were moving on to casting. The director, Cora Huang, already had the lead actors in mind and reached out to them. She would be working with a casting director for the remaining roles. Jihae and Colin had brief phone calls and exchanged emails, but hadn't seen each other since they interviewed the directors together. Both of them acted as though they were business partners and nothing more.

But wasn't that the truth? They *weren't* anything more than that. Sure, they'd shared two passionate kisses, and Colin looked at her like he wanted to tear off her clothes whenever he thought she wasn't watching him—she smiled smugly at the thought—but that didn't mean there was anything between them.

Jihae gnawed at her lip. She wasn't a woman who opened up easily, and physical acts weren't meaningless to her. Those kisses had meant something to her and it irked her that Colin was able to ignore them so casually.

When she heard a knock at the door, she shook her head to clear it.

"Come in."

June stuck in her head. "Hey, boss. I'm taking the team out to dinner—on you, of course—to show them how much you care."

"That's great, and I do care. Too bad it wouldn't fit my image to join you guys. Besides, if I come along, the staff will be so tense, they'll probably get indigestion," Jihae said, only half joking.

"Hey. You could come if you want," her friend said with gentle sympathy. She understood Jihae's isolation and loneliness.

"No, I've got work to do. You guys go and have fun," she replied with a forced a smile.

"Are you sure?"

"I'm sure. Now go away. I really have to work."

"Fine. Do you want me to lock up for you?"

"No, I'll lock up on my way out."

"Okay. See you tomorrow, friend."

When the door clicked shut, Jihae had the sudden urge to run after everyone. *What happened to cool professionalism, Princess?* She was in an odd mood and blamed it on Colin Song. Jihae wouldn't be feeling so lonely if she'd never known how warm and cherished she felt in his arms. She tsked impatiently. *Stop being unreasonable.* Pushing Colin from her thoughts, she turned her attention to her inbox.

Confidential: Top Priority jumped out at her from the top of her unread emails. It was from her father, which startled her. He usually left emails and such to his executive assistant. With trepidation, Jihae clicked open the email, and what she found inside befuddled her.

Introduce Yami Corporation's CFO to one of your contacts at NAM.

That was it. The terseness was expected but the content made no sense to her. She'd never heard of Yami Corporation. If she had to guess, they were an apparel company. She might've seen a bus-bench ad featuring a model wearing their jeans.

She wasn't directly involved with Rotelle Corporation's businesses, but she had some knowledge of which companies they did business with. Yami wasn't one of them. Besides, fashion was one of the few industries that Rotelle didn't dabble in. Why would Father want her to introduce Yami Corporation's CFO to a talent agency?

None of it made sense. She checked the time and calculated that her father might be awake. He was something of an insomniac.

"Father," she said when he picked up after a few rings as expected.

"What is it?"

"Your email. It doesn't make sense."

"It's not your job to understand but to do as I instructed you," he said dismissively.

She forged on despite his tone. "Since when did Rotelle do business with Yami Corporation? Isn't that an apparel company? We don't do apparel."

"You don't know everything. Far from it."

"I don't *want* to know *everything*. I just need to know why Yami's CFO wants an introduction to NAM."

"How the hell should I know? Just do as you're told and stop wasting my time with incessant questions." His terse tone warned her that she didn't have much time.

"My connection to the talent agency is important for my job. For Rotelle Entertainment. I can't jeopardize it by pushing a stranger on them for reasons unknown."

There was a brief pause as he considered her words, and Jihae's grip on her phone tightened.

"You can deal with the details of the introduction directly with Yami's CFO. If she tries to ask you questions relating to Rotelle Corporation, tell her you don't know anything. Which is the truth. You're merely my representative." He sighed quietly. "I need someone I can trust to handle this."

Her father sounded so weary that her heart constricted. "I understand, Father. I'll take care of it."

"Good."

"Father…" She hesitated, wanting to ask him if he was okay. The line went dead before she could say another word.

While she doubted there was any information, Jihae searched the internet for any connection between Rotelle and Yami. Not surprisingly, she found nothing. What she did find left a bad taste in her mouth. Yami Corporation had competed against Hansol for a partnership with Vivotex. The mention of Hansol still brought with it a twinge of humiliation even though she had cheered on Garrett Song in her head. He had been brave to marry the woman he loved rather than marry the woman chosen for him by his family. She closed the browser window resolutely. She didn't care what Yami had to do with Hansol.

The office was empty but the door was unlocked, so there was someone still there. Colin hoped that someone would be Jihae. He'd assiduously avoided her since the director interviews—he had Ethan and Kim deal with anything that required direct contact— but he knew that this cowardly tactic couldn't last forever. He and Jihae were partners. They needed to work fluidly together without a middleman.

No matter how much her presence tempted him,

he had to keep his attraction to her separate from CS Productions business. With the director selected and the casting underway, it was past time to discuss their future direction and to prioritize what had to get done. He told himself that was why he'd rushed to her office after hours, as he stood in front of her door.

Just as he was about to knock, he heard the murmur of her voice. He turned away thinking she was in a meeting or on the phone. But her next words froze him to the spot.

"Since when did Rotelle do business with Yami Corporation? Isn't that an apparel company? We don't do apparel."

After a moment's pause, she continued, "I don't want to know everything. I just need to know why Yami's CFO wants an introduction to NAM."

Colin couldn't hear the other side of the conversation, which meant she was on the phone. His heart pounded against his chest, and sweat sprung out across his hairline. Yami Corporation wanted an introduction to NAM? And Jihae was supposed to do the honors? Why?

"My connection to the talent agency is important for my job. For Rotelle Entertainment. I can't jeopardize it by pushing a stranger on them for reasons unknown," she said.

For reasons unknown. The sudden elation caught him off guard. Blood pounded in his ears, and his chest rose up and down as he fought for his breath. Jihae knew nothing. His gut instinct hadn't steered him wrong. She hadn't been involved in the espionage. Colin had been worried that his judgment was compromised by his desire for her, but now he had proof of her innocence. The relief made him light-headed.

"I understand, Father. I'll take care of it."

Then trepidation washed over him. Was Rotelle scheming again? Her father was instructing her to meet Yami's CFO, and she'd just agreed. She might not know anything yet, but the meeting might get her involuntarily involved. He didn't want her taken down with her father just because the conniving snake decided to embroil her in the mess now. But the Jihae he knew would balk at any shady business. Her honesty and integrity wouldn't allow her to do anything she felt was wrong. He trusted Jihae. She would be smart about it, and keep herself safe.

And Rotelle Corporation would be taken down. After running into dead end after dead end, the investigation was about to get a fresh start. After tugging his cell phone out of his back pocket, Colin typed in a quick text to Garrett.

Found new lead on Rotelle. Yami's CFO might be their contact person. Have PI shadow her.

Then he turned his phone to mute. The professionals could handle the rest. He'd carried out his duty to his family, and he could stop scrounging around for evidence. A part of him whispered that he still might need to keep an eye on Jihae, but he hushed the nagging voice. His belief in Jihae's innocence hadn't been wishful thinking born out of his interest in her. She truly was innocent. He didn't need to feel guilty for having feelings for her—the Song family's enemy—anymore. His careening thoughts came to a screeching stop.

Did he have feelings for her? *Yes*. Colin cared about Jihae. He'd been suppressing his feelings and calling it lust because caring for her would've been a betrayal of his family. But now, with proof of her innocence, he could let himself admit his feelings for her. And maybe even act on them.

Colin took a deep breath, then knocked softly on Jihae's door. He was being either brave or stupid, but he didn't want to hold back. Not anymore.

"Come in?" she said after a brief pause.

"I hope I'm not interrupting anything," he said as he walked into her office, closing the door behind him.

"Colin." His name left her mouth in a breathy whisper, and her wide eyes revealed her pleasure at his unexpected appearance. But it disappeared with a blink. Her damn armor was back in place. "What are you doing here?"

She looked pristine in her white Princess Jihae attire, but her cheeks were stained with color and loose strands of hair framed her delicate face. He had never seen a more beautiful sight. Her expression exuded confidence and a hint of tightly controlled curiosity, but her eyes greedily roamed his body. Despite his rejection and subsequent inattention, Jihae miraculously still wanted him, but it was going to be diffi-cult to have her admit it again. What was it she'd said?

I will have you on your knees before I ever let you lay a finger on me again.

With the last traces of his suspicion gone—freeing him from any guilt he might have felt over betraying his family by wanting her the way he did—he saw her with clarity for the first time. Her intelligence, her integrity, her beauty, her courage to experience new situations with curiosity and joy. He respected her. He desired her. And he wanted to do much, much more than lay a finger on her.

She'd come to stand in front of him as he stood glued to the spot, gazing mutely at her. With her within arm's reach, her exquisite scent hit him, jerk-ing him out of his paralysis. He wanted to kiss her so badly a shiver shook his frame. But if he wanted to kiss her, he had to get on his knees. She was quite clear on that, and he intended to obey her explicitly.

His expression must have shifted because her eyes widened and she took a hasty step back. Her retreat snapped the last of his control, and he stalked her step by step until she was backed against the wall.

"I asked what you're doing here," she said with the slightest catch in her voice and lifted her eyes to meet his. "I don't believe we have any urgent busi-ness at the moment."

"Oh, you're wrong about that," he growled. "I have *very* urgent business with you."

Her pink lips parted on a gasp before she stood up straighter. "And what business is that?"

He lowered his head, gaze darting over her lovely face, until her eyes fluttered shut. But rather than claiming her mouth, as he was badly tempted to do, he brought his lips close to her ear and whispered, "Come with me."

Before she could answer, he leaned back and took her hand in his own. When he walked toward the door with single-minded determination, Jihae came willingly until she stopped short. Colin's stomach dropped to his feet. He didn't know if he could handle her rejection tonight.

"Wait," she said softly. "I need to get my purse and lock up for the night."

He nodded jerkily, both relieved and impatient. He freed her hand so she could lock the door, but placed his hand possessively on her lower back. Once she was finished, he reclaimed her hand. He couldn't bear not touching her for even a moment.

"Where are we going?" she asked when he settled into the driver's seat beside her.

"My place." He was amazed that he could still get words out. His heart was hammering against his chest and his hands trembled as he backed out of the parking space.

"Your place?"

He gave a curt nod and kept his eyes on the road. Jihae didn't voice any objections and settled into her seat, turning her attention out the window. Her face was carefully expressionless, so he couldn't guess what she was thinking, but Colin was grateful that she was coming with him.

By the time they arrived at his condo, his hands were shaking so badly that he had trouble unlocking his door. This was a bad idea, but he was all out of willpower.

"Would you like a drink?" he asked as casually as he could once they were inside.

"What have you got?"

Jihae reached down to remove her heels, bracing a hand on the wall. He couldn't help noticing how shapely her calves were. He had groveling to do before he could let his thoughts go anywhere near there. He snapped his eyes back to her face, but it wasn't much help because it was also distractingly beautiful.

"Everything," Colin said with a wry grin. "My cousin is an amateur mixologist and insisted I needed a full bar for when she visits."

"Is she good?"

"She's an amazing cook but her cocktails taste like fruit-infused diesel fuel."

Laughter trilled out of Jihae as he led her toward his wet bar. To his surprise, she removed her suit jacket and handed it to him, and began rolling up the sleeves of her silk shirt.

"You don't seem like a harsh critic at all," Jihae said with a mischievous smile. An odd ache came and went in the recesses of his heart at her playfulness. He liked this side of her so much. "Well, no matter. I do love a challenge."

"You're an amateur mixologist, too?"

"Actually, I'm a professional." She laughed at the shock on his face. "I took a crash course in bartending and have a certificate to prove it. I actually have a shoebox full of cooking, baking, flower-arrangement, you-name-it certificates. I snuck in bartending as my little rebellion against my parents' will to domesticate me before my wed—"

Before her wedding. The thought of her having almost married Garrett made his jaws clench. But not wanting her to feel flustered, he quickly redirected their conversation. "So are you planning to wow me with your skills?"

"Depends. Can I raid your fridge?" she said, her relief evident in her smile.

"Be my guest. I have to warn you, though. There isn't much in there."

He followed her into his kitchen and leaned against the island as Jihae searched for ingredients.

"Aha," she said, straightening up with a basket of blueberries and a serrano chili pepper.

"You're using those blueberries?" he asked with his forehead furrowed in consternation. "Are they still good?"

"A little dry, but perfectly edible. They'll do fine for my needs. But…" Her eyes darted around the kitchen counter.

"Do you need something else?"

"You don't happen to have any basil, do you?"

He actually had a miniature herb garden. Another gift from Adelaide. She claimed that even if he couldn't cook worth a damn, adding some fresh herbs into premade sauces did wonders.

"Um…this way, please."

Colin showed her to the little alcove where his garden of basil, Italian parsley and thyme flourished under artificial sunlight.

"You have an herb garden?" she said with an incredulous smile.

He scratched the back of his head and shrugged. "It's here to help me with my abysmal cooking skills."

"Aww, I think that's rather sweet." She reached out and gently grazed the herbs with her fingers.

"Really?" he said, breaking into a wide grin. "I'll take that."

Once they were back at the wet bar, Jihae got to work. With quick twists of her wrist and fast-moving hands, she muddled the basil with some blueberries and a splash of simple syrup, then poured the mixture into the shaker. Then she added measures of fragrant gin and elderflower liquor into it, and topped it off with ice before she shook the shaker with easy efficiency.

A glint of mischief entered her eyes, then she bumped the shaker from elbow to elbow before throwing it and catching it behind her back. It was an exciting finale. Simple and elegant. Especially when done with her intoxicating half smile. She added a slice serrano chili into two martini glasses and poured the concoction into them.

It was hot. She was hot. *Damn.*

She pushed a glass toward him and raised hers in the air. *"Gun-bae."*

"Gun-bae." While the salutation meant "bottoms up" in Korean, Colin took a much more careful sip of

the drink. His eyes widened and he gawked at Jihae. "Why aren't you out there selling this stuff? How about if I buy the recipe from you for my clubs?"

"Is that what I'm doing here? Having another business meeting?" She took out the sting in her words with a teasing smile.

"Dammit. Sorry. No."

"Relax, Song. My claws are officially withdrawn," she said, raising her curled fingers toward him like little paws. "Besides, I just made the drink up on the spot, so there is no recipe. I'd probably forget it in like two minutes."

Colin gave her a pained look. He didn't want to sound like a haggling businessman tonight, but it would be a travesty for the rest of the world to never try her cocktail. He didn't know what to do, so he bit his lip and stayed quiet.

Jihae's laughter filled his living room as she took him out of his misery. "Give me a pen and paper. I'll jot down what I remember."

He patted his pants for a piece of paper and found a receipt, then grabbed a pen. "Here."

She turned over the receipt and bit the end of the pen. Then she wrote out the recipe for him. She paused, worrying her bottom lip, then smiled as she scribbled something on top. She handed him the receipt with a look of anticipation in her eyes.

"Once in a Blue Moon," he read, and looked up to smile at her. "Clever."

"I figured I won't be coming to your condo to create brilliant cocktail recipes very often—"

"No," he blurted, cutting her off in the middle of the sentence.

She cocked her head in question. "*No* what?"

"No, I want you to come to my condo often—very often—and mix as many amazing drinks as you'd like."

"I don't understand."

"Be with me, Jihae."

Nine

"Colin, I..." Jihae couldn't continue because he pressed his index finger against her lips.

Slowly withdrawing his finger, he came around the bar and clasped her hand, then tugged her toward his couch. She couldn't breathe. What was he doing? Well, she had a vague idea he hadn't brought her to his condo to talk business, but she wasn't sure what exactly he wanted.

"I want you, Jihae."

With gentle pressure on her shoulders, he settled her on the couch then he kneeled in front of her, spreading her legs to get as close to her as possible.

"But..." She didn't know what she meant to say as the heat in his eyes sucked the air out the room. All she could recall was that she'd told him he would need to get on his knees if he wanted to touch her again. And here he was. On his knees. She was going to have a heart attack.

"May I kiss you?"

"I don't know. Why now? What's changed?"

Colin blinked rapidly as though her question had touched a nerve. Before she could wrap her mind around it, he replied, "Me. I've changed. I want you, and I can't hold back anymore."

He wanted her and he was finally admitting it. Sweet victory. A triumphant smile rose to the surface, and she wet her already tingling lips. "So…you want to kiss me?"

"Very much."

She had no patience left to gloat because she wanted to kiss him very much, too. Jihae wrapped her arms around his neck and lowered her face toward his. She dropped a chaste kiss on the corner of his mouth. "Like this?"

"More," he growled, his hands spanning her waist.

With a whisper of contact, she moved her mouth from one corner to the other. "Like this?"

"More." His fingers tensed around her waist.

"Show me," she commanded into his ear.

He moved so fast that she gasped against his lips as they crushed against hers. His kiss wasn't gentle or teasing. It was Colin's desire bared raw. Their teeth clacked as his tongue danced with hers, demanding that she match his passion. She had zero problem with that. His hands traveled to her hair and made quick work of undoing her bun. When her hair was free, he tangled his fingers into the long strands and tilted her head to expose the column of her neck.

His hot breath and wet lips drew a line down to her collarbone and the hollow at her throat. He licked and blew into the sensitive spot, and she moaned helplessly.

"Colin."

He hastily captured her lips again as though to swallow her small sounds of pleasure, his name on her lips. She scooted farther back into the sofa and lay down, pulling Colin on top of her. When all of him covered all of her, he groaned his approval.

She wanted him naked. She wanted him to fill her. She whimpered and writhed under him when his thumb brushed the tip of her aching breast. He pushed up her shirt and her bra, exposing the hard tip, and sucked it into his mouth. She nearly screamed and knew she was close to losing all control.

"Wait," Jihae gasped, pushing against his shoulders.

"Wait?" Colin immediately raised his head and looked her in the eyes with heavily hooded lids. *Gah. Sexiest bedroom eyes ever.* She almost pulled him back against her breasts, but she took a deep breath instead. Or at least she tried.

"Yes, wait. Please," she said, barely managing to get the words out.

She was so turned on, and so was he. Colin sat up on the couch and pulled her onto his lap as though he couldn't quite break contact with her. He smoothed her hair out of her face and said, "Tell me. What is it?"

"You and I... We're both doing this against our better judgment. True?"

"True," he replied with a bemused curl of his lips. Then he kissed her temple with such tenderness she wanted to melt against him. "Continue."

"To ensure we don't regret this, I think we should set some ground rules." When Colin nodded for her to continue, Jihae placed a kiss on his jaw. "Rule One, this—us... We have to be discreet. I don't want this to affect our professional reputation in any way. And I absolutely don't want my father to find out. This has to stay between us, and us alone. Okay?"

"Okay."

His eyes had turned watchful at the mention of her father, and she cringed in embarrassment. Bringing up her father while warm and horny in Colin's arms was not the sexiest of maneuvers.

"Rule Two, no matter where this leads, I want us to finish our project together. I won't sacrifice *Best Placed Bets* for anything."

"Agreed."

"Rule Three, no promises. I want us to take this one day at a time. Let's just be two adults, enjoying each other."

Jihae knew herself. What she felt for Colin wasn't commonplace. Not for her. If she slept with him, she might give too much of herself to him. She couldn't allow that to happen. She wasn't even in the States permanently. Once their project was finished and her father summoned her home, she would have no choice but to return to Korea. To return to her family and her duties.

"No promises," Colin said solemnly while he quietly searched her face. Afraid of revealing her vulnerabilities to him—and how much she wanted promises—she buried her face against his neck. "May I add something?"

Surprised, she pulled away to look at him again. "Of course."

"While we take this day by day, I want all of you for every day we have together. I don't like to share."

She sucked in a sharp breath at the possessive note in his voice and nodded rapidly. "Okay. And same goes for you."

"Oh, don't worry about that. You will have my complete and undivided attention while we're together. There won't be room for anyone or anything else."

Hot damn. She wanted to fan herself. He said "complete and undivided attention" with such intensity, she could only imagine what making love to him would be like. But ironing out the rules made things suddenly seem so real that Jihae was overcome with shyness.

"So, um, what should we do now?" she asked. She wanted to palm herself in the forehead. It sounded like "should we shag now?" She truly wasn't trying to be suggestive.

"I have an idea or two," he said in a low voice that sent shivers down her spine.

All shyness forgotten, she took his face in both of

her hands and kissed him until they were both out of breath but hungry for more. Desperate to be closer to him, Jihae straddled his lap and pushed herself against him, delighting in the pressure of his hard chest against her aching nipples.

It wasn't enough. She shifted back just enough to get her hands between them and began unbuttoning her blouse. Making a noise of frustration, Colin pushed away her fumbling fingers and undressed her himself. Once the blouse was pushed down her shoulders, he reached around her and unclasped her bra. After he'd thrown that on the floor, he immediately took a hard, sensitive peak in his mouth. Moaning with exquisite pleasure, she instinctively ground her hips against his hardness.

"God, Jihae," he said as he freed one nipple and moved on to the other. "You're killing me."

"Perfect," she replied in a small puff of breath, giddy with relief and joy.

"Oh, is it?" He pulled back to grin wickedly at her, and she squirmed in her seat so he could go back to what he was doing so beautifully. "I'm going to get you back for that."

"What—"

Before she knew it, Jihae was lying on her back on the sofa with Colin kneeling at her feet. "I'm going to make you come so hard, you'll scream."

Jihae wasn't sure if she was excited or a little alarmed. Probably both. She was already so wet and aching, she didn't know if she could take any more.

When he parted her thighs, nestling his head between her knees, her hands fisted in his hair.

The first lick and hot breath had her whimpering, "Please."

Other than a low, rumbling chuckle, Colin didn't stop to respond. He licked her center with slow, sensual attention until she was a mass of desire. When he added a finger, then another, she ground against his hand and tongue without self-consciousness. Only want. She was so close that she could see white sparks beginning to go off behind her lids. Somehow sensing she was about to fall off the edge, he pulled her into his mouth and gently sucked.

"Colin." His name left her lips in a sharp scream and her hips lifted off the sofa.

He pushed her hips firmly against the cushions and brought her down torturously slow, his palm lightly massaging her sensitized core. Once she could see straight again, Colin rewarded her by removing his shirt and pants in swift succession. When he was gloriously naked, he took a foil packet from his wallet, tore it open with his teeth and sheathed himself.

His eyes looked out of focus and heavy-lidded with need as he smoothed the hair out of her eyes. "You okay?"

"Yes, I just need you inside of me," she said, biting her bottom lip. "Please."

His gaze not leaving hers, he plunged inside her, deep and heavy. She felt herself stretching to accommodate him.

"God. You feel so good," he said.

"So do you." But it wasn't enough. She swerved her hips to get used to the feel of him.

"Wait. Don't do that," he groaned. "I'm close to losing it just being inside you. I want to take it slowly."

"Colin, I've been wanting this from the moment I saw you," she said, shifting in the other direction, and was rewarded with his hips jerking involuntarily against her. "Screw taking it slowly."

With a helpless groan, Colin pulled himself out and buried himself to the hilt inside her. Then out again and deeper still. She matched him thrust for thrust until all semblance of a smooth rhythm broke down and they jerked wildly against each other, each seeking a climax so close within reach.

"Yes. God, yes." She fell apart, with him close behind, pumping wildly into her before shouting his own release.

Colin collapsed on top of her, but shifted slightly to the side on his elbow so he wouldn't crush her. Her limp legs hung over his back and one of her arms hung loosely off the side of the couch.

"My God," she whispered in a raspy, awe-filled voice. "That was brilliant."

"Anytime, sweetheart," he replied, his voice muffled, his shoulders shaking with laughter against her. After a moment, he raised his head to look into her face. "It was my absolute pleasure."

That was the most amazing, mind-blowing sex she'd ever had, but he managed to make her want him again with just a crooked smile and a few husky words. She wanted this after-sex warmth to last, but realized they would soon have to untangle their limbs and get off the couch. Then what? Would he expect her to leave right away? No, he wouldn't be that callous; he'd said he wanted this to be a real relationship, at least while it lasted.

So, putting aside her trepidation, she simply asked, "Do you want to watch a movie?"

"Absolutely," he said as he shifted his weight off her.

"Perfect." Jihae must've sighed in relief because a knowing grin spread across Colin's face. "I mean, good. I'm glad."

"Here." He handed her the remote control, then began picking his clothes up off the floor. "You choose the movie and I'll pop the popcorn after I clean up."

Colin was sweet and considerate, and she sighed dreamily. She wasn't going to hope for an unattainable future, but would enjoy the here and now to the fullest. Because the here and now was pretty fantastic.

Colin had been wearing a stupid grin on his face all day. He and Jihae were dating. It was a secret, and it belonged only to them. *Hell.* He was a grown-ass man, acting like a giddy high-schooler. If he hadn't been buried in work, he would've been drawing heart curlicues on his notepad. Fortunately, the sheer size of his workload prevented him from making an even bigger fool of himself.

To be discreet, they hadn't appeared in public together more than once a week, and they were even more careful about spending time at each other's places. They took advantage of as many chances as possible to see each other in their business capacity, but it was a far cry from spending time alone with her. The curtailed opportunities for privacy were frustrating, but it made each meeting all the more precious.

The script was close to being finalized—it was even better than his highest expectations—and the auditions were scheduled to commence in the next month or so. Other than relaying the author's suggestions to the director, he and Jihae would be relatively hands-off in the initial creative process. They trusted Cora, and the casting director she brought on board, to do an amazing job.

But they definitely wanted to be present when the candidates for the female and male leads did their readings. In a romantic comedy, the hero and heroine's chemistry was crucial to whether the movie worked or not. They wanted sparks coming off the lead actors when they were together on screen. Cora had some strong favorites she wanted to work with. He and Jihae also saw great potential in her choices, but they wouldn't know for certain until they saw the candidates read together in person.

He leaned back in his chair and stretched out his stiff neck and shoulders. The clock on his monitor told him it was already past seven thirty in the evening. *Damn.* He'd wanted to mix business with pleasure with Jihae tonight, but she might already have had dinner. He sat upright and texted her, his pulse picking up speed.

Hungry?

Her response was almost immediate. I'm starving, baby.

He choked on a laugh even as his shifted uncomfortably in his chair. He loved her sexy sass.

I could fix that. What about for food?

Hungry for that, too.

Then allow me to fix that, as well. Where should we meet?

Somewhere that serves cheesy, decadent pizza.

He gave her the name of the perfect place for her craving. She was a bit closer to the restaurant than he, so he only had time to write one more email before he closed shop. That minuscule act of discipline made him feel a bit more in control of himself, and he was able to stop himself from running to his car.

Despite his attempts to slow down, he arrived early at the restaurant. He always came before Jihae. Not that she had a habit of running late, but he simply enjoyed the anticipation of waiting for her arrival, with his heart pumping a little faster each passing minute.

When she finally walked into the restaurant, his stomach clenched in a visceral reaction to her presence. She was wearing a white pantsuit with a pale, off-white blouse. Her patent-leather, nude stilettos completed her signature look. She exuded aloof so-phistication and ice-cold detachment. He couldn't be-lieve how well she carried off her public image when he knew how contrary it was to her true personality.

"You look lovely," he said softly into her ear while pulling out her chair.

"Thank you." Her expression remained carefully neutral but a splash of pink stained her cheeks.

"This place has the best New York-style pizza you'll find on the West Coast." He took his seat across from her and opened up his menu.

"Yum. I'm starving."

"So you've said," he drawled, staring pointedly at her perfect red lips.

"Now behave." She arched an eyebrow at him. The subtle twitch at the corner of her lips betrayed that she was holding back a smile.

"When have I not?" Other than tugging her into a stairwell the last time they'd met to kiss the hell out of her only to find the door locked behind them. They'd had to climb five stories to find an open door. And that other time… Now that he thought of it, he'd misbehaved quite a lot.

Jihae gave him the subtlest eye roll in the world. Actually, he only recognized it as an eye roll from spending so much time with her. Her every emotion and expression was subdued to the point of stoicism in public, but he soaked up her barely there smiles and the teasing twinkle in her eyes that were meant only for him.

As dinner progressed, however, Jihae's subtle

smiles and gentle teasing grew dim, and her eyes took on a distracted, faraway look every time there was a slight pause in their conversation.

"Hey," Colin said, reaching across the table to touch her hand. But he hastily withdrew as soon as he realized what he was doing. PDA was not a risk they wanted to take. "Is everything all right? You're hiding it well, but you seem distraught. We could talk about it in private later, if you'd like."

"No, everything is fine. I'm fine. I'm just knackered." She looked down at her pizza and pulled off a pepperoni to pop in her mouth. "I had a three-hour meeting with the Korean production team on one of our celebrity reality shows. They're a well-oiled machine but it was a lot to catch up on."

"That must've been draining." She was hiding something from him, and nausea rose in his throat. Was it about her meeting with Yami Corporation's CFO? He hadn't heard back from Garrett about the PI's progress, and it'd been weeks. "Once you finish your pizza, we'll get out of here. Okay?"

"That'll be nice. Thank you." But again, her smile fell short of reaching her eyes.

"Should we go to your place, so you don't have to go out again?"

"No," she said in a rush. "I mean… I'd like to go to your place tonight."

"Sure. We'll do that."

They were quiet on the drive to his condo, each of them lost in their own thoughts. What was she hiding from him? More than ever, he believed her innocence.

Throughout the film production, Jihae was always the first to ensure that everything was aboveboard. If there was ever the slightest doubt, she would err on the side of being shortchanged rather than injure the other party. The Jihae he knew would never involve herself in any unethical behavior, much less corporate espionage. But something had happened today and he wanted to find out what. Was it about Yami Corp.?

Once they were inside, he helped Jihae out of her jacket and hung it in the entryway. She stepped out of her heels with a sigh and plopped herself down on the sofa like a limp doll. He couldn't fight the smile that pulled at his lips. He loved it. He loved how she just let go and relaxed when she was alone with him.

He followed her to the sofa, pulled up her legs onto his lap and gently massaged the ball of her foot.

"Mmm. You're good at that," she said, her eyelids fluttering shut.

"I'm good at a lot of things," he joked, moving on to the arch.

"And ever so humble."

He tickled her for that response and nearly got kicked in the jaw. "Whoa, watch it. You could've broken something."

"Sorry. I seriously could have," she said, breathless from laughter. "I'm really, *really* ticklish."

"That doesn't sound right." He ran his hand up the back of her legs. "I've touched you everywhere and you haven't reacted like this before."

"Just on my feet. I'm only ticklish there."

"Thank goodness. Otherwise, I'll get a good beating every time we make love."

"Aw, poor Colin. Did I scare you? We could take a break tonight if you want."

"Not on your life," he growled, pouncing on her. "I already don't get to have you often enough. I wouldn't stay away from you even if you were covered in sharp needles."

She giggled and pretended to push him off her, but he made quick work of trapping her arms above her head. "Can we at least go to your bedroom tonight? I feel like we rarely make it that far before we rip each other's clothes off."

"As you wish."

He stood from the couch, lifted her into his arms and carried her into his room. After laying her down on the bed, he unbuttoned and shrugged out of his shirt as Jihae watched with rapt attention. As he unclasped his belt, a familiar ringtone sounded from his back pocket. Garrett. And all his trepidation from earlier in the evening rushed back to him.

"God, I'm sorry," he said, pulling out his phone. "I need to take this."

"Go right ahead. I'm not going anywhere."

Colin left the bedroom and walked into his study, making sure to close the door behind him.

"Garrett."

"Hey, little cousin. What are you up to? You sound a bit out of breath. Did I interrupt your workout?"

"In a manner of speaking, yes. So, what's going

on? Any news on the lead?" Colin deliberately exhaled when he noticed that he was holding his breath.

"As a matter of fact, there is, but I thought we might exchange some social niceties like normal people first."

"Since when do the Songs engage in small talk over the phone?"

"I guess you have a point." Garrett chuckled on the other end.

"So tell me. Was there any movement from Yami Corporation?"

"Yes. Yami's CFO, Sylvia Taylor, finally met with Jihae Park at a coffee shop this afternoon."

Colin's heart drummed against his ribs. "Did we have ears on them?"

"Our PI had someone planted a couple tables away."

"What—what did they talk about?" he asked, both eager and afraid to hear the answer.

"The conversation was convoluted and brief. Taylor asked Jihae Park about how her father was doing and whether Rotelle was running smoothly. Park effectively shut her down and asked for the reason she wanted an introduction to NAM."

"Then what?"

"Taylor said her father owed her, and Park should just do as she was told."

Colin almost laughed. Jihae would not have liked that. "What happened next?"

"She told Taylor in no uncertain terms that there

will be no introductions to the talent agency unless there were legitimate reasons for it."

Atta girl. "So, did Taylor succumb and tell her everything?"

"Basically, but nothing of use to us. She wanted Park to pressure executives at NAM to have their big-name stars endorse Yami Corporation's apparel. Be seen wearing it and share how much they love it on social media. All for free."

"That's ridiculous. Jihae would never ask for something like that from NAM. She values them as colleagues."

"I guess Taylor thought NAM would rather do Park's bidding than lose Rotelle Entertainment's goodwill."

"That may very well be true, but Taylor wanted to take advantage of NAM. It's far from a fair deal. Jihae would never stand for that."

There was a short pause. "You sound pretty confident about that."

"I am." Colin clenched his fists, ready to defend Jihae if his cousin questioned her integrity.

But all Garrett said was "Huh."

"What is that supposed to mean?"

"It means *huh*. Why does it have to mean anything?" There was a smile in his cousin's voice. Was Colin that obvious about his feelings for Jihae? "Anyway, the only information that we gleaned from their meeting was that Sylvia Taylor believes Chairman Park *owes* her. Just more circumstantial evidence."

"So how did the meeting end?"

"Park told Taylor to go pound sand, and Taylor left in a huff, threatening that her father won't be happy about this. Maybe Taylor has something on Chairman Park and is pressuring him for favors. But could she be so foolish as to anger the chairman? If she was, then she was playing with fire. The bastard might humor her for now, but he will bury her for daring to pressure him." Garrett's sigh communicated his frustration across the line. "But again, it's all speculation and conjecture. We got nothing, which means we're back to square one."

"We did get something. This meeting proves that Jihae Park is innocent. She obviously doesn't know what Rotelle Corporation's connection to Yami is about. She was forced to play the middleman, but she walked away."

"Again, it's all just conjecture at this point, and it isn't Park's innocence that we're trying to prove but Rotelle's guilt."

But it wasn't conjecture. Jihae could've inadvertently been pulled into the espionage scheme, but she'd distanced herself from the situation. She was innocent but the situation reeked of her father's guilt.

"So what's next?" Colin dragged his fingers through his hair, pacing his office.

"We need to continue keeping an eye on Sylvia Taylor and Jihae Park."

"On Jihae? She's not a part of this."

"We don't know that for sure. She may even be the key to solving this case."

Colin blew out a frustrated breath, not liking the

idea of Jihae being watched. It could also reveal their relationship, but he would deal with that later. He needed to protect Jihae from being under the PI's surveillance.

"Look, Garrett. I'm sure Grandmother has relayed to you that I'm working with Rotelle Entertainment while keeping an eye on Jihae Park. From everything I've seen so far, I believe her innocence. But if she ever diverges from that, I'll be there to see it. Jihae is already under casual surveillance by her father's people. Following her would only risk the PI's cover and expose our investigation."

"I see your point. Then we'll leave Jihae Park up to you and focus on Taylor." There was a slight pause on the line. "Colin, I appreciate you doing this for the family, but be careful. You don't need to risk your dream for us or Hansol. If things get too hot, I want you to stop and focus on producing your film. Is that a deal?"

"Deal." A small smile quirked Colin's lips. Garrett was like an older brother to him, and he appreciated how he always looked out for him. "Thanks for the advice, *hyung*."

The weight on his shoulders feeling significantly lighter, Colin walked back to his bedroom. Jihae was asleep exactly where he'd left her. She slept with her hand tucked under her chin like a child. He could imagine touching her skin and finding it hard and cold as porcelain, she was so perfect in her sleep. Then her pouty lips blew out a soft breath that sounded like *puuuu*.

He wasn't quick enough to cover up his snort but managed to hold back his laughter with his hand over his mouth. He loved that sound. It was so adorable. She always did that—blew out puffs of air like she was trying to extinguish a row of birthday candles— when she was especially tired.

Still laughing softly, he tiptoed to the dresser and searched for a blanket, since she was sleeping over the duvet. He pulled out a soft knit throw and laid it gently over Jihae's sleeping form. He badly wanted to climb into bed with her and hold her as she slept, but no alarm would wake him if he got that cozy. Frustratingly, sleepovers weren't allowed in their secrecy pact, so he would need to wake her up in a couple of hours to send her home.

Colin walked to the kitchen and got some coffee going. He would stay awake and catch up on some work. Then he would provide Jihae with the most erotic and satisfying wake-up service she'd ever had.

Ten

"Sylvia Taylor is trying to leech off NAM and their clients. I'm not a brainless pawn you can push around," she said in a commanding tone she'd never used with her father. "I know I haven't been a perfect daughter to you, but if you see me as an intelligent human being, you have to let me make my own decisions."

"You have always been too soft. And stubborn. If you are aware that you've disappointed your mother and me, you should obey me without question."

It didn't come as a surprise that her father would take a hard line with her. But that didn't mean she was going to take it lying down.

"Why are you so set on helping Ms. Taylor?"

"Who says I'm set on helping her? You don't need

to know anything other than the fact that I want you to do this favor for Taylor. I am keeping you in the dark for your own good."

"No. I refuse to do it." Jihae's heart pounded so loudly she was afraid she wouldn't hear her father's response. She had never outright defied her father except for her rebellion after college.

"Then I will remove you from your position at Rotelle Entertainment effective immediately." It wasn't an idle threat. He wouldn't hesitate to take away what was most important to her. Unless it wasn't in his best interest.

"I'm in the middle of a production with a partner company. If you remove me now, the partnership and the production will suffer, as well as the film itself. I know my company and my teams better than anyone else. Are you willing to gamble with Rotelle Entertainment's success after everything I've built up? How happy do you think the shareholders will be at my sudden dismissal? You can't deny that Rotelle Entertainment is one of Rotelle Corporation's most profitable branches."

"You overestimate your value. Rotelle Entertainment is profitable because it's a part of Rotelle Corporation. But I am too busy to deal with finding your successor right now." That was his way of capitulating without giving her credit. He knew that Rotelle Entertainment would falter if he removed her before the film was complete. "I will allow you to remain as the head of Rotelle Entertainment for the time being, but don't fool yourself into thinking your disobedience will go unpunished."

"Oh, no. I would never doubt your ability to hold on to a grudge." Jihae gasped behind her hand. She couldn't believe her own recklessness.

"Such impudence! How dare you speak to me this way?"

She needed to appease him if she wanted to hold on to her position at Rotelle Entertainment. Jihae had to keep her promise to Colin and see *Best Placed Bets* to its completion with him.

"I'm truly sorry, Father. Please forgive me. The stress of being on bad terms with you has made me hysterical. I still can't introduce Yami Corporation to NAM, but please let me keep my current job. I only want the best for Rotelle Corporation."

He took a huffing breath on the other end of the line. Jihae smiled bitterly. Her groveling had done its job. With his ego stoked and her pride in tatters, he was going to give her an inch. "Like I said, you can remain in your position for the time being. But what happens after that depends on how you deal with Yami Corporation."

And that was the end of the call. She listened to the dial tone for a blank moment before sluggishly putting down her phone. Production was going smoothly, and so was her relationship with Colin. It was going so well that she sometimes forgot Rule Three—no promises—and dreamed of more. The call with her father was a rough intrusion of reality. She would be returning to Korea sooner rather than later. That much was certain. Her defiance in the Yami situation had cemented that outcome. But she would never change her mind about the introduction. What Yami intended to do was contemptible and she would have no part in it.

Her father was hiding something from her. If he was desperate enough to get her involved in the first place, it was something very big. It was time she dug for some answers. She pushed back from her desk and poked her head out the door.

"Hey, do you have time to have dinner tonight?" Jihae asked.

"I'm not sure. Let me check my very busy social calendar," June replied, pretending to flip through a calendar. "I would have to move a couple things around, but I can squeeze you in."

"Does Korean barbeque and soju at my place sound good?"

"Pork belly from that butcher on Third Street?"

"Hell to the yes."

"Meh," June said, deadpan. "I'm not holding back on the soju, so plan on making it a dinner-slash-sleepover."

"Done deal."

Jihae closed her office door and walked back to her desk. It would be wonderful to vent about her father to her best friend and figure out a way to uncover his secret. The only reason she wasn't grinning from ear to ear was that she had to cancel her date with Colin. They've been together for a few months, but she still couldn't get enough of him. But taking a break tonight was for the best. The mess with her father and her eminent return to Korea meant it was a bad idea to get more attached to him. She needed to create a cushion to protect her heart.

Despite her decision to distance herself a bit, it still hurt not to see him tonight. Rather than torturing herself more by calling, she texted him instead.

Hi.

The ellipses appeared on her phone immediately.

Hi.

I need to cancel our date tonight.

This time the ellipses took a while to pop up.

Is there a particular reason?

Yeah. Emergency girls' night in.

Is there something wrong?

Not really. Well, there's something. I'm just having some daddy issues that I need to vent about to June. She knows my history.

She stopped herself from explaining any further. She had every right to hang out with her friend. But Colin's answer brought a smile to her lips.

I hope it isn't anything serious and you could still have a fun time with her.

Not to worry. We'll have fun. It would be hard not to with pork belly and soju in the mix.

Don't do anything I wouldn't do.

I can't make any promises, she typed without thinking.

There was another pause from him, and she realized that she'd inadvertently brought up their no-promises rule. She hadn't meant to fling that out like a defensive mechanism. While she wanted to maintain some distance, she didn't want to remind him that they weren't meant to last. Was she overreacting? Colin probably never even thought of having something long-term with her.

She wanted to tell him that she would miss him. She missed him so much already, but heartfelt confessions weren't conducive to not forming an attachment.

After they texted their goodbyes, she tried to focus on her game plan to dig in to her father's secret. Jihae had people she trusted within Rotelle Corporation, but she wanted to avoid asking them to outright spy on their own company. She would have to figure out a legitimate way to have them look for a connection between Rotelle and Yami Corp., no matter how minuscule. If she didn't know about it, it wouldn't be easy to find, but her people knew how to open doors.

If they found nothing then she would have to play

a dangerous game, and get June involved in her mission. But that had to be the very last resort. It involved using June's connections in Rotelle's accounting department to follow the money. With her father, money was always the focus of any situation or problem. Whatever he was keeping from her had to involve payment of some sort, and no matter how deeply it was buried, someone from the inside should be able to unearth it.

But Jihae was terrified of what she would find. And it was the ultimate act of rebellion against her father. What if she discovered something bigger than she could imagine? She wanted the truth, but she didn't want to put any of her friends in danger of being disciplined by the company. Hopefully, her friends in high places would be able to sniff out some minor scandal, and she wouldn't have to get June involved.

She pressed the heels of her hands into her eyes. It was too much. She wanted to forget about her suffocating life, and the strangeness that was seeping into it. To forget that she would soon have to leave Colin. She wanted the world to fall away as she fell apart in his arms, where nothing mattered but the two of them being together.

A humorless laugh escaped her. She was the one who'd decided to cancel the date. She was the one who needed the reminder that their relationship was finite. But now all she wanted was to wrap herself around him and hold on. Hold on tight.

She stopped herself short. *Bloody hell.* How long

had it been? How long had she been on the precipice of falling in love with Colin? The frightening part was that despite everything—including her guaranteed heartbreak when she had to leave him—she wanted to let herself fall.

Colin was becoming an expert at creating legitimate business reasons to spend alone time with Jihae. The latest and most brilliant idea was this location-scouting trip. It wasn't just an excuse to get away together. It was an important part of the production. They'd been discussing the possible location for a scene they both loved.

"I'd never been on a road trip," Jihae said in a singsong voice as she adjusted her sunglasses. She had her legs up on the dashboard and the sun glinted off her pink-tipped toes.

"So you've mentioned…about six times in the last couple hours," Colin teased. She leaned over and delivered a decent punch to his arm. "Hey, there will be no abusing the driver. I'm guessing you're new to road trips, so you may not be aware, but distracting the driver is a no-no."

"It is?" she asked in a suspiciously innocent voice.

"Yes. A big no-no." He shot a quick glance at her to see what she was up to, but she just gave him a wicked grin.

"So…let's say I unbuttoned myself, like so." She undid the top button of her thin, loose shirt. Then reached for the next button. "Then unbuttoned another one, like so. Would this be considered distracting the driver?"

"Not at all," he growled through clenched teeth. "By all means. Make yourself comfortable."

Her laughter felt like a caress down his body, and he frowned harder. How did he always manage to get into these situations with Jihae? She was relentless and he was helpless against her bold moves.

"Then I'll just undo one last button, so the top of my white lacy bra peeks out. Oh, look! It's your favorite one."

"You know I'll get you back for this."

"I don't know what you mean… I'm new to road trips and just don't know how to behave. Am I being bad?"

"As soon as we check into our hotel, and I hang the Do Not Disturb on the knob, I'm having you against the door."

"What the hell?" The top of her chest, exposed through her unbuttoned shirt, turned pink as color traveled up her neck. "It's all right for the driver to turn on and distract the passenger? That's a double standard. Who made up these ridiculous road-trip rules?"

Helpless laughter escaped him, affection tangled up with frustration. He reached out and patted her thigh, his fingers a hair's width short of the inseam of her pants. "Don't worry. You'll get the hang of it."

"Ugh. You're incorrigible," she said, squeezing his hand before she slapped it away.

Colin drove the next three hours with blue balls

and anticipation rushing through his veins. When they at last entered Death Valley National Park, the sun had begun its descent, painting the sky and mountains with splashes of red, orange and violet.

"This is brilliant," Jihae breathed, leaning forward in her seat to look out the windshield.

"It is. The rest of the park is spectacular but you can't beat the sunsets against the mountains." He turned into one of Death Valley's two hotels. "So are you ready to rough it for two nights? We're on the same travel budget as location scouts, so the accommodations won't be up to your usual standards."

"I've stayed in *hostels* before." She crinkled her nose at him. "A standard room in a four-diamond hotel isn't roughing it."

"When did you stay in a hostel?"

"Around seven years ago."

"But what kind of accommodations do you usually have?"

"Presidential suites and penthouses. Fine. I get your point. You don't have to rub my nose in it. I never asked to live like a spoiled princess," she said glumly. "So how do *you* rough it, Mr. Self-Made Millionaire?"

"I usually camp when I come to national parks."

"Camp?" Her face held both horror and fascination. "Like as in camping? In the outdoors?"

"Wait a minute. You can't be serious." He turned to stare at her after parking the car. "You've never gone camping?"

"You probably don't know a lot about my family,

but my father isn't exactly the type to load the family into the car and go camping," she said a little wistfully. Colin shrugged to hide his discomfort, because he did know quite a bit about her family. Before he could think of an appropriate response, she continued, "But I do want to try it."

"I'll take you someday," he said before he could think.

Did she think he was making her a promise? That they would be together long enough to reach *someday*? Maybe they *could* have their *someday*. He could come clean to her. Every moment he'd spent with her had been real. His every word and every touch had been true. But no. It was too late. She would despise him if she found out about his identity and how he'd betrayed her trust.

"Let's see if I could survive a couple nights in a standard room," Jihae said with a small, sad smile that broke his heart. "Besides, I don't think *Best Placed Bets* has a camping scene."

During the check-in, Colin requested adjoining rooms, so they could spend the night together without sneaking back and forth. When they got to her room, he was the perfect gentleman, opening the door for her and placing her suitcase just inside the entry.

"I'll see you later," he said, and left Jihae with her mouth gaping. Once he let himself into his room, he promptly found the entrance to hers and knocked. He heard shuffling and a muffled *oof* before she flung open the door.

"Hi." He grinned at her wide-eyed expression.

"Is that your room or the rest of my room?" she asked, getting on her tiptoes to look over his shoulder.

He laughed, and stepped aside to invite her in. "Welcome to my room."

"So this *is* the whole room," she said, excited about the new experience.

"Sure is."

Her eyes took in his room, identical to hers, in a quick sweep, then pressed herself against one wall. Then she took measured strides until she reached the opposite wall and burst out laughing.

"You could walk from one side of room to the other in less than twelve steps. It's so small and cute."

He walked over to her—in ten steps for him—and leaned down to nuzzle her neck. "I'm glad you like it."

"Mmm-hmm. I do. It's so fun." She leaned her head to one side to give him better access. "And I love our connecting door. We could finally have a sleepover."

He placed his hands on her waist and walked her backward until her back met the door that led to the hotel hallway. She gasped in surprise and stared at him.

"For real?"

"Hell, yes," he said before he crushed his mouth against hers.

Jihae's surprise was short-lived as she eagerly pressed her body against his and deepened the kiss, urging him to respond. He growled deep in his chest, his desire for her bursting into dangerous flames.

He reached between them and ripped open the

blouse she'd carefully unbuttoned in the car. Impatient to taste her, he pulled down her bra until her breasts came free. He took her in his mouth until she moaned, digging her hands into his hair. He suckled deeply then moved greedily to her other breast, his hands reaching behind to cup her round backside.

Her hands tugged and tore at his shirt. He leaned back only far enough to pull it over his head, then reclaimed her lips. He shivered as she explored his chest and stomach, and smoothed her hand lower.

"God," he groaned. "I need to be inside you."

Rather than answering, she hurriedly unbuckled his belt and pushed down his jeans, then made short work of her own pants. He ran his hands over her naked body then stepped away to sheathe himself as quickly as his trembling hands would allow. Desperate beyond coherent thought, he wrapped her leg around his waist then lifted her up and brought her down on him, tilting his hip so he was buried inside her to the hilt.

"Colin."

"Yes, baby. Talk to me."

"Faster."

Her breathless demand pushed him over the edge and he pounded into her again and again without even a pretense of control. He was so damn close, he wasn't sure how much longer he could last.

"I need you to… I don't know if I can… Jihae, please."

He shifted her in his arms to give her more contact where she needed it and pumped harder, willing her to come. Just as he thought he wasn't going to make it, she screamed, tilting her head back against the door, eyes clenched shut. He joined her in climax and pushed into her one final time.

His limbs still trembling, he gently lowered Jihae's feet onto the floor and leaned against her.

"I've been dying to do this to you for hours," he mumbled against her warm, smooth neck. "You make me so crazy."

"And I can't get enough of you," she said huskily, her hands moving up and down his sweat-slickened back, both soothing and arousing him.

"We're going to shower first then I'm taking you to bed. Then we'll order room service to replenish ourselves, and go again. I'm not letting you out of my arms until tomorrow morning. Thoughts?"

"Oh, just that we're going to need to order a ton of food."

Eleven

Jihae opened her eyes slowly, savoring the feel of Colin's body wrapped around hers. Waking up next to him felt so right. She had never felt such warmth and security before. She wanted more, but this stolen night was the only chance they had to spend in each other's arms unless they could plan more location hunts without making everyone suspicious. Not only that, it also wasn't right using project funds to pay for their rendezvous.

She sighed, clutching at the arm Colin had wrapped over her. She shouldn't be worrying about having more of him, but making the best of what she had now. And right now, she had a hot hunk of a man, naked in bed with her. Letting go of her desperate hold on his arm, she reached behind her and wrapped her hand around him. *Mmm.* She smiled with her eyes closed. He was already hard.

"Hi, are you awake?" she whispered, slowly pumping her hand up and down his erection.

"You're insatiable, woman. Not even letting me rest after a long night," he growled, his hand sliding up to cradle her breast.

"From the state you're in, you've hardly had enough yourself."

"No, I haven't. I don't know if I ever will."

He flipped her to face him and swiftly took her mouth in a hungry, plunging kiss. They'd gone from zero to sixty in two seconds flat. She frantically swept his body with her hands, wanting to touch him everywhere at once. When he responded in kind with a pained groan, she had no room for anything in her mind but Colin and the way he touched her.

Their pleasure grew and consumed them, and soon their shouts of pleasure filled the room. They lay limp and satisfied while trying to catch their breath. Her lazy gaze drifted to the clock on her nightstand and she sat upright.

"It's eight o'clock! I thought you wanted to get an early start."

"You're right. Let's take a shower together to save time and get out there."

"You have to promise to behave in the shower otherwise we're going to lose more time."

"Scout's honor."

They hardly fooled around at all in the shower, and got ready in good time. After grabbing some coffee and muffins from the coffee shop in the lobby, they set out on the scouting adventure.

The proud peaks of the valley surrounded them as they drove from one point of interest to the next. South Korea was a beautiful country with four distinct seasons, each bearing its own fairy-tale charm. But she had never seen or experienced anything like the great vastness of Death Valley. One thing after another amazed her: standing in the Badwater Basin, 282 feet below sea level, driving through the spectacular desert hills of Artist's Drive and the aptly named Artist's Palette, a geologic kaleidoscope of colors, and enjoying a handful of hiking trails. Each point of interest held its own unique charms, and she would never forget any of it. Especially since she got to experience it all with Colin by her side.

"I think we have the hiking trail we want." He took his eyes off the road for a second to glance at her. "Do you want to see one more spot? It's spectacular during sunset."

"What is it?"

"Have you seen *Star Wars*?"

"I beg your pardon?" she said with an affronted stare. "How could you even ask that?"

"Sorry. Sorry. So you must know what Tatooine is."

She rolled her eyes and didn't grace him with a response.

"Well, they filmed the Tatooine scenes for *A New Hope* and *Return of the Jedi* here in Death Valley.

The Mesquite Flat Sand Dunes is probably the most recognizable of the locations."

"Shut. Up." She swiveled toward him and said in a near shout, "Are you bloody serious? Yes! I want to see Tatooine."

The sand dunes rose and fell in endless waves against the backdrop of the jagged, rocky hills and the bright orange-and-yellow sky. It was freaking Tatooine.

"Let's go, let's go," she said as she jumped out of his car. She took off in a run, not waiting to see if Colin was following her. Every person to themselves. They were on Tatooine, for God's sake.

She was out of breath by the time she reached the top of the first hill. But she got to enjoy the view of Colin climbing the hill with his backpack filled with their supplies. Always prepared. When he reached the top, he handed her a water bottle.

"Drink, you nut. We're literally in a desert. Don't let the cool air fool you."

"Yes, sir." She winked at him and chugged at her water. She actually was very thirsty after the climb. "Let's keep going."

They were sandy and sweaty by the time they returned to the car, but Jihae didn't mind it one bit. That had been glorious. They even got a nice couple to take a picture of them together. It was the only one she had and it made her heart clench because she'd cherish it when this was all over.

They drove back to the hotel in serene silence, taking in the surroundings and the changing colors of the sunset. When they reached their rooms, Colin turned to her and bowed formally.

"May I take you out to dinner tonight?"

She giggled coyly into her hand and replied in her poshest British accent. "That would be an absolute pleasure."

"Excellent. I have reservations for seven. Is that enough time for you to rest and get ready?"

"Sure, as long as we take some alone time and take separate showers."

Colin laughed, dropping his silly formality. "I guess I could bear to stand an hour and a half on my own."

Jihae, on the other hand, felt a twinge of regret at not getting to spend every minute with him, but she needed to rest a bit. More importantly, she wanted to surprise him with the new dress she'd brought. She wanted to look beautiful for him.

"I'll see you soon," she said.

Their gazes held until she closed her door. Despite her best intentions, she was tempted to fling open the door and say *Just kidding. Of course I want to shower with you.*

After taking a shower *alone*, she sat down on her lonely king bed and switched on the TV, mostly for the commercials. She grabbed the brush she'd set down on the nightstand and methodically brushed out her hair. When her feet and legs felt a little less tired, she got up to blow-dry her hair. She planned on wearing it down for Colin. It went against the Princess Jihae rules, but they were far from home. No one was going to capture a picture of her and post it on social media out here.

Once her hair fell like dark satin down her back, she took time with her makeup, painting her eyes with dramatic colors. She kept her blush to a minimum and applied a deep pink lip stain to her lips.

She withdrew her dress from the garment bag and stepped into it. It was a rich, emerald-colored strapless dress with a fitted top and a tulip skirt that fell halfway down her thighs. She chose clear, crystal-dotted heels to complete the outfit. The mirror told her it had been worth the effort to dress up for Colin. She was still her, but she looked more like the fun, vibrant person she could be with Colin. It was an amazing feeling to see her outside appearance match the person she was inside. She couldn't wait to see the expression on Colin's face.

A quick glance at the clock told her she'd made it with five minutes to spare. She waited patiently for one more minute, then grabbed her clutch and headed out the door. There was no rule that a man had to pick up the woman, right?

When she knocked smartly on his door, she heard him walking toward it. She was holding on to the doorframe with one hand, arm raised high above her head, and leaning into it in her best Hollywood-bombshell pose. She felt a little silly but it was fun, and she wanted to have a bit of fun tonight.

"I… You…" Colin stared slack-jawed at her. His eyes heated as they traveled down her body then back up to her face. "Hell."

"Hmm. I was fishing for a compliment. But I'll take 'I… You… Hell,' I guess."

"If we didn't have a reservation, I would pull you into this room and make love to you with your hot little dress pushed up to your waist. You look so beautiful. I won't be able to undress you later."

She gasped softly, her own body warming and softening to his words. She coughed indelicately into her fist and fought for her composure. She had wanted to wow him, and had succeeded, but it was still a rush. As calm returned to her, she noticed he was handsome as hell in his blue suit and fine gray shirt. She could just about eat him up.

"Turn around," she said, biting her lower lip.

"What? Why?"

"Because I want to see what those pants do to your fine ass."

With a shrug, Colin turned in a slow circle for her. He raised an eyebrow with an arrogance that made her body burn. "Do I meet your approval?"

"Yes." She cleared her throat. "Top marks. Excellent bottom, that."

His low chuckle made her want to forget about the dinner reservations, but this kind of *real date* was not easy to come by. In fact, this was their first official date. She wasn't going to shortchange herself on it.

He stepped out of his room and offered her his arm. "Shall we?"

"Yes, please." She took his arm and smiled into his eyes.

The dining room was charming and intimate, and

Colin had a romantic table by the fireplace reserved for them. He ordered them red wine—she was more of a craft-beer aficionado—then reached across the table and placed the tips of his fingers on her hand for a brief second.

"You're so beautiful," he said.

"Thank you," she said with a deep blush, suddenly feeling shy.

"I wish…"

"What? What do you wish?"

"I wish… I could have something I can't have."

"What is it? Tell me." She looked intently into his eyes, holding her breath. He seemed to be on the precipice of something monumental, and by the way his gaze bore into hers, it had to do with her. Did he want promises? A future with her?

He shook his head as though to clear it, and laughed lightly. "I wish we could fly to Lake Como and spend a lazy week there. Work has been so hectic for so long, I could really use a break. But alas, *Best Placed Bets* has no scenes set in Italy, so we wouldn't have any excuse to go."

He had been about to say something else. She knew it, and he wisely, but disappointingly, had taken the safer route.

She forced a bright smile and said, "Lake Como sounds wonderful. I always wanted to go there, but it was a bit far for my graduation trip."

The food was fresh and elegant, but she didn't taste much of it. The fun, romantic date she'd been hoping for now had an undercurrent of tension and melancholy. Colin was quieter than usual, too.

When they went to bed that night, he made love to her with an intensity that made her heart ache, like he was memorizing every single part of her. It felt as though he was preparing to let her go. In her head, she knew that it was for the best since she had to do the same, but everything in her being screamed that it couldn't be—that they had to be together.

It was hopeless. She was hopeless. She had gone and fallen in love with Colin.

"Are you well, Hal-muh-nee?" Colin said, as he kneeled on a *bang-suk* on the hard floor. He came to his grandmother because he was too lost to find his way back on his own.

Death Valley had been a few months ago, but he still dreamed of waking up with Jihae cradled in his arms, soft and warm in her sleep. He wanted to wake up beside her every morning. At some point along the way, he'd allowed himself to dream that she could be his forever. But now he wanted it to become reality.

"I am, but I don't think you could say the same," his grandmother replied, concern drawing her eyebrows together. "Sit comfortably, and tell me what has you so distressed."

Now that he was in front of his grandmother, he didn't know where to start. He had screwed up so royally, he didn't think even she could help untangle him from the mess of knots.

Colin had made himself a part of the investigation of Rotelle Corporation's espionage scheme. He'd helped rekindle a cold case by effectively spying on Jihae. Their relationship, at least on his part, was built on lies. But the lies and omissions had to stop. He had to find the courage to tell her the truth—all of it—and hope to God she would give him a chance to make it up to her. To make her happy.

"It's about Jihae," he said, rubbing his aching chest with the heel of his hand. "No. It's about me."

Grandmother gazed steadily at him with a calm countenance, patiently waiting for him to continue.

"I shouldn't have kept my identity a secret. It was cowardly and manipulative. I should have convinced her that she should work with me despite the fact that I'm a Song." He looked down at his fisted hands. "Now I'm in love with her, but everything we have together has been built on my lies."

"Does the girl know that you love her? Does she care for you?"

"I don't know. I think she cares about me, but once she finds out who I am and what I've done, she'll despise me for it."

"If that is truly the only outcome, then why are you here?" she asked with a shrewd glint in her eyes. "You are here because you want to correct the mistakes you have made."

"I do. I want to tell her the truth."

"What is really holding you back?"

"I'm afraid I'll lose her when I tell her the truth. Not only that, but I would be asking her to choose between me and her family. Her father would never allow her to be with me. If she stays me then she will lose her family and Rotelle Entertainment."

"Is it fair to ask that of her?" his grandmother said.

"It won't only be my deception I'll reveal to her. To tell her the whole truth, I'll have to tell her about her father's attempts to sabotage Hansol and destroy Garrett's marriage. Will she want to stay with her family knowing that? Maybe I won't have to ask her to choose between me and her family."

"Hmm. Don't you think she might use her knowledge of your deception against our family? To let her father know that we are on his trail?"

"No. Absolutely not. Jihae is honest, fair and principled. She'll never help her father, knowing what he had done. My gut told me from the beginning that she was innocent. And I have proof that she isn't involved, if you still have doubts."

"Yes, yes. I know what you overheard from her conversation with her father and how she refused to help Yami Corporation's CFO. Besides, you don't need to convince me of her innocence."

"But I do, Hal-muh-nee. I want you and Uncle James, and the rest of the family, to accept her. She is truly an amazing person, but so lonely. Her family…they aren't like us. They don't love her and appreciate her like family should. She's been neglected, controlled and used by them. I want her to become a part of our family and be loved as I have been. I want you to accept her as your own."

"Colin, do you want to marry this girl? Is that what you're telling me?"

"Yes. I want to marry her and make her happy. I want to beg for her forgiveness and make up for any hurt my lies will cause her when I tell her the truth."

"Then is it fear? Is it only fear that is holding you back from telling her the truth?"

"You're right. I'm so afraid of losing her, Grandmother. I can't bear to even think about living my life without her in it. If I tell her, she might leave me. Maybe I want to delay the inevitable."

"But you said you love her. Every day you continue to keep this secret, the more you are hurting her. Is that what you want? Is that the right way to love her?"

"I've been lying to myself that I'll be able to let her go when the time comes. That neither of us is emotionally involved, and we'll be able to walk away from each other without heartache. I've been so wrong." He wiped both his hands down his face, hating himself a little. "If I love her, I have to give her the choice to leave or stay based on the whole truth. If she wants to leave me after I've told her everything, she has the right to make that choice. If by some miracle, she is willing to give me another chance, then that is her choice, as well. Telling her the truth and respecting her decision is the best way I can truly love her at this point."

He pushed away the nagging thought that even if Jihae gave him another chance, her father wouldn't back down easily. If Colin ever reached that point, he would fight the world for her as long as she stood beside him.

"Colin, I know you. You are a good man. You

made a difficult choice based on the difficult situation you were placed in. I know that my desire to have you join Hansol has been a great source of stress and guilt for you. In that, I feel partially responsible for your decision to spy on Rotelle Corporation. I understand you did that to pay me back a debt you don't owe me. You have done the best you can for our family."

"None of this is your fault. It's all mine. I had a choice and I made the wrong one. But now I understand what I have to do," he said with determination. "Hal-muh-nee, will you do something for me?"

"Anything, my dear child."

"If Jihae is willing to have me, will you promise to make her a part of our family?"

"If she will have us, then she will be family." She reached out to squeeze Colin's hand. "She will be my granddaughter."

Twelve

Jihae ended the call on her cell with shaky hands and placed it on her desk with a clack. She knew her father was a ruthless businessman, but she never thought it possible that he would be willing to break the law to get what he wanted.

Her friends from Korea had gotten back to her with disturbing news. They'd dug up some stale rumors among the highest executives that Rotelle Corporation might have planted a spy in Hansol Corporation the previous year. It didn't tell her how Yami Corp. was involved in the espionage, but her gut feeling said this was the secret her father had been keeping from her.

But why? Why would her father do this? He had more money than ten generations of his descendants could live off. Anything else he earned was superfluous other than for feeding his pride. Jihae froze. His pride.

She had a nagging feeling about the timing of the spy being planted. The rumors had sprung up almost a year and a half ago. Close to the time that Garrett Song had broken his engagement to Jihae.

Oh, my God.

All that time, her father had blamed her for the broken engagement. That it had happened because word of her *unruliness* got out. He had blamed what she'd done as a college kid to guilt her for her broken engagement. And like a prat, a part of her had believed him. She'd believed that it was her fault. And she'd beat herself up for losing the chance to gain her freedom from her family. Soon, she'd regained her senses and was relieved the arranged marriage hadn't happened, but she still had carried her guilt inside her, trying to appease her father.

But behind all that censure, he had committed corporate espionage to get revenge for his humiliation. He couldn't stand that a mere nouveau riche family had dared to refuse his daughter's hand. So he'd taken out his frustrations on his jilted daughter and had gone after Hansol where it would hurt the most.

He hadn't been able to keep his crimes a complete secret, based on the rumors floating around among the inner circle. Her father, with his brilliant, conniving mind, must've known that his crimes could be revealed. And that was where Jihae came in.

He'd timed her business trip to the United States so she would be present for the commencement of his espionage plans. And his recent attempts to get her involved in dealings with Yami Corp. all seemed too perfect to be coincidences. Her involvement now would make her the perfect fall guy. That was why he'd been so adamant that she meet Sylvia Taylor and make the introductions she demanded. It might've even been her father who'd offered Jihae's services to Sylvia Taylor to fabricate a direct connection between her and Yami Corporation.

All the evidence would point toward her—the woman scorned who'd sought revenge against her ex-fiancé and his family. She was the one in the United States. And if she'd blindly done what her father had demanded, she would be the one who went out of her way to help Yami Corporation. It would look like Jihae was trying to appease Sylvia Taylor because she had something on her. Then her father could claim to have no knowledge of the crime, and accuse Jihae of doing everything behind his back. There was no better scapegoat than his own daughter.

Devastation seared her heart black, and she shivered uncontrollably. She hugged herself tightly and clenched her jaws to keep them from chattering. She'd thought he loved her in his own way. She was his daughter, after all. But wasn't this proof of what she'd been denying all her life? Her father didn't love her. At least not enough to take the fall for his own crimes.

Her heart was breaking and her world was falling apart, and she could only think… *Colin*.

She needed him. Her shaking would only stop when his arms were wrapped around her. Silent tears were falling down her cheeks, soaking the front of her shirt. With jerky movements, she reached for her cell phone.

Colin. I need you. Please, she typed after several attempts.

What's wrong? What is it? Are you okay?

Just come. Please.

Are you at the office?

No, I worked from home today.

I'll be there in twenty minutes.

The mere fact that he was on his way eased some of her shivering, but she couldn't make her limbs work. So she sat very still at her desk, not bothering to stem the flow of tears. She didn't have the will to make them stop. She couldn't don her stiff upper lip, like Princess Jihae should.

In what seemed like both a second and a year, keys jingled and her door opened. Even though they were always together when they visited each other's places, they had exchanged their keys just in case. It was a good thing since her legs wouldn't hold her long enough to have stood up and opened the door for him.

"Jihae." Colin came thundering in, his hair standing in peaks and his eyes wild with worry. When he spotted her at her desk, he rushed to her side and kneeled beside her. He held her face between his warm hands as the tears continued to fall. "What is it? What's wrong, baby? Please tell me."

There was so much—so much that needed to be said. But now, she only wanted him and to forget everything else. By some miracle, she managed to whisper, "Hold me, Colin."

He wrapped his strong arms around her without hesitation, and he held her head tucked into the crook of his neck. He murmured soothing words while his hand drew reassuring circles on her back.

At some point, he lifted her into his arms and carried her to the sofa, then nestled her on his lap. The murmurs and the gentle touches didn't stop. She couldn't remember how long they stayed like that, but at some point, her tears finally ran dry and she clutched at the front of Colin's shirt.

She'd been abandoned by her father in the worst way, and she couldn't lose Colin, too. There was no family for her anymore. Even if her mother hadn't been part of her father's scheme, she would never oppose him for Jihae. She was alone and had no obligations, responsibilities or duties to make her return to Korea. Rotelle Entertainment was as good as lost since she'd disobeyed her father. But she had the experience and connections to start fresh in Hollywood. Losing Rotelle Entertainment didn't frighten her anymore. As long as she had Colin, she could face anything.

"I love you, Colin. I love you so much." She wanted

promises. She wanted forever with Colin, and she didn't have to hold back anymore.

"Jihae." He tensed under her, his Adam's apple bobbing as he swallowed. "You can't say that. Not yet. Not right now. You're hurting, and there are things you should know..."

All she needed to know right now was that she loved him. That she'd finally found the courage to tell him she loved him. Talking could wait. She placed the tips of her fingers on his lips.

"Whatever it is, it doesn't matter. I don't want to hear it. In fact, I don't want to talk, either. All I want is you. Right now. Make love to me, Colin. Make me feel whole."

He gently pulled away her hand and looked at her with such sad eyes that it frightened her. "Jihae, I have something to tell you."

She didn't want to hear why he had such sorrow in his eyes. She couldn't handle any more bad news today, so she grabbed his face with both her hands and brought his mouth down to meet hers. He stiffened and tried to pull away, but she straddled him and swept her tongue across his bottom lip. When she swiveled her hips against him, he capitulated with a helpless groan and kissed her back with dark, stormy passion.

Their mouths met and dueled, and their teeth bit and teased. They frantically tore off each other's tops, and Jihae spread her hands possessively over his broad, muscular chest, then leaned back to admire his beautiful body. While she was distracted, Colin threw her bra to the floor and palmed her breasts and massaged them.

She moaned and ground her center against his hard length until he echoed her moan and leaned in to kiss the sensitive spot behind her ear.

"Colin, please," she said, grinding her hips harder while hot moisture soaked through her panties.

He hiked her skirt to her waist and grabbed and tore her lacy lingerie in half. With fumbling hands, she helped him unbuckle his belt and unzipped him, pulling out his erection. She wrapped her hand around it and moved it up and down, drawing a groan from him.

"Condom," he rasped, lifting his hip off the sofa. "Back pocket."

The shift of his hips tore a high-pitched moan from Jihae, but she quickly reached down, pulled out his wallet and found the condom. When he grabbed for it, she shook her head. She tore open the package with her teeth.

"No, let me," she said.

As soon as she covered him with the condom, she pushed herself up on her knees then sank deep onto him. Colin made an attempt to check his passion and started out at a slow tempo. But she didn't want slow. This coupling was about her claiming him. Marking him as hers.

She pulled herself up and came down with a rotation of her hips. He scrunched his eyes shut and hissed, as though in pain. So she did it again. Faster and harder. She kissed him and her tongue mimicked the movement of her hips.

"I'm going to take you fast and hard, darling," she said against his lips. "And you're going to fall apart under me, screaming my name."

"God, you're killing me."

"Am I?" She emphasized her question with two hard pumps. "Tell me you're mine."

"I'm yours, Jihae."

"Tell me I'm yours." This time his response faltered, so she sank into him even deeper, circling her hips until he groaned. "Tell me I'm yours."

"You're mine. God help me. You're mine. Mine alone."

His eyes opened then and he grabbed her waist and lifted her up, tilting his hip into her. He filled her so deeply and fully that she whimpered, her smooth tempo falling apart. Colin took over with a fast, desperate rhythm, his movements hard and inelegant. Jihae was going to be sore later, but it felt so good. So right. There was nothing for her to do other than push him even harder.

She was so close, but she wanted to prolong this moment, so she hung on.

"Come on, baby. Come for me. Come for me, baby."

His pleading words were almost enough to push her over the edge, and when he sucked her aching nipple into his hot mouth, she came apart, atom by atom.

"Colin." Her scream echoed through her living room.

He was pushing faster and faster into her, his movements becoming more erratic by the second. A hoarse shout escaped his throat as he jerked into her one final time. They sat there cradling each other as they came back to earth. Her condo was still and quiet except for their harsh, shallow breaths.

Then, in a broken voice, Colin whispered, "I love you, Jihae."

"I love you more than anything, baby." His voice caught in his throat as his heartfelt admission tore free of him.

This wasn't how it was supposed to happen. As soon as he'd left his grandmother's house several days ago, Colin had gone to pick out an engagement ring. He was an optimistic son of a bitch. Knowing her kindness, her goodness, he'd let himself hope that maybe he had a chance of keeping her. That somehow she would forgive him and give him another chance. If she were to forgive him, he didn't plan on wasting a single second with her. He was going to propose to her.

But the timing hadn't been right the last few days. They'd worked long, hard hours, and by the time they were alone together, they were too exhausted to talk. And today she'd been so scared and suffering. When she'd told him she loved him, his heart burst inside him and set off beautiful fireworks of hope.

He was supposed to tell her that he loved her first. After he'd told her the truth, he was supposed to beg her for forgiveness and offer her his love. He didn't want her to feel humiliated by his duplicity any more than necessary. But now, with her love out in the open, she was going to feel doubly humiliated. Doubly betrayed.

He should have told her sooner. Much sooner. He had been a coward and now the little hope he had might be blown forever.

Once their breaths returned to normal, he gently sat her to the side and brushed her hair out of her eyes.

"I need to clean up. I'll be right back," he said.

She smiled tremulously and nodded.

He was a goddamn bastard. He went into the guest bathroom and stepped under the shower. He let the hot water wash over him, wishing it could wash away his guilt. But what was done was done. He couldn't change that, but he would do the right thing tonight.

Colin found her in the kitchen, holding a steaming mug of tea. Her hair was wet and tucked behind her ears, and she looked cozy in her pale blue pajamas. She glanced at him from beneath her lashes, suddenly shy.

"I made you some tea," she said, pointing to a steaming mug on the island.

He took a seat in front of it and motioned for Jihae to sit beside him. As he gathered his courage to reveal his secrets, she said in a soft, faraway voice, "I just found out today that my father was a criminal, and he had been planning to set me up to take the fall for his actions."

"He what?" Colin roared. She didn't deserve that.

Her bastard of a father didn't deserve Jihae. He took a deep breath to calm himself. "Are you all right?"

"Don't worry. He *tried* to set me up, but failed. I acted out of character and didn't obey him down to the letter. I'm safe. Legally." She turned wide eyes to him, cocking her head to the side. "Aren't you going to ask me what this is all about?"

He attempted to swallow and failed, then answered, "I think I know exactly what this is all about."

"What are you talking about? How could you know any of it?"

"Will you promise to hear me out? Will you give me a chance to explain?"

"You could tell me anything. What's going on, Colin?" she asked, putting her soft hand on top of his trembling one.

"I'm Colin Song."

"Yes, and I'm Jihae Park," she said lightly, but unease crept into her expression.

"I am Colin *Song*, one of the heirs to Hansol Corporation, and Garrett Song's cousin."

She'd picked up her mug to sip her tea, but it came crashing down on the island, shattering against the marble. "What are you saying? I don't understand."

"Careful," he yelled. "You're going to hurt—"

She didn't hear him, or she didn't care. She pushed herself up to her feet with her hands on the counter. A jagged piece of the mug cut a bright line in her tender palm, but she didn't even flinch.

"Tell me!"

"Please, baby. You're hurt. Just let me stop the bleeding on your hand, and I'll tell you everything."

She backed against a wall and lifted her bloody palm to ward him off. "Stay where you are. Don't you dare come near me."

"Jihae—"

"Tell. Me. Now."

He needed to do as she asked if there was any chance of calming her down.

"I kept my identity a secret from you because I wanted you to see CS Productions on its merits. My team shouldn't suffer the burden of my connections. My family has nothing to do with CS Productions."

"You thought your cousin's jilted fiancée couldn't possibly know the difference between personal life and professional life?" Coldness seeped into her voice, but at least she appeared to be calming down. He suspected the next part would shatter that calm again.

"There was more than that. Rotelle had planted a spy in Hansol Corporation that could have derailed Garrett from becoming the CEO. Despite our PI's best efforts to figure out the extent of the espionage so the family could bring a legal case against Rotelle, the trail had run cold. And I wanted to find out something helpful for the investigation. I wanted to help my family find justice."

"So you lied to me to avenge your family. In your eyes, I was already guilty by association."

"The spy your father recruited through Yami Corp. was Garrett's wife's former lover. He had set it up so

Natalie would take the fall for the espionage. Garrett nearly lost his wife and daughter because of that. Because of the way your father attacked Garrett and Natalie so specifically, we didn't doubt you were involved."

Blood drained so completely from her face that her lips matched her pale skin. "That's because my father is very thorough in his deviousness. If evidence of the espionage attempt somehow led to him, he set it up so that I would take the fall for it. He'd even timed my arrival in the States to match the commencement of his scheme."

"Did you find that out today? God, that bastard. How could he do that to you? I'm so sorry—"

"Shut. Your. Mouth. You have no right to be sorry for my father's betrayal when *you* betrayed me so thoroughly. You *used* me."

"I was an idiot. I thought I was doing it for my family. To pay them back for their love and support." This was a nightmare. He was drowning in fear, and he couldn't see the light above. "But from the day I started working with you, I knew in my gut that you had nothing to do with the espionage scheme. Then you confirmed in your conversation with your father that you didn't even know who Yami Corp. was—"

"You actually spied on me? You listened in on a conversation I was having with my father? Which conversation was this? Since you discovered I didn't know who Yami Corp. was then…that was my first conversation with my father about Yami and the whole mess. That was the night we first made love."

She gasped and speared him with a look of such accusation and heartbreak that he had to look away. "Did you make love to me—have this relationship with me—to earn my trust? Was all this your way of using me to get information out of me? Or was it your plan to break my heart all along? To avenge your precious family?"

"Jihae, no. God, no." He took a step toward her and she flinched, turning her head away as though his proximity would hurt her. He stopped. "I made love to you because I couldn't hold back anymore. No matter how hard I fought it, I wanted you more than my next breath. Not being with you would have burned me into ashes."

"So the part where you had sex with me was just to satiate your lust then."

"No. Please. I knew in the depths of my soul that you were innocent, and by relaying Sylvia Taylor's move to Hansol's PI, my involvement in the investigation was over. I didn't know then, but I was already so deeply in love with you. I fooled myself into thinking that I would be happy with whatever you gave me. I didn't deserve forever with you, but I thought we could have a short time together without you getting hurt. I was an idiot and none of it makes sense now."

"No, it doesn't. You were selfish, and you were cowardly."

"I was, but I will make it up to you if you would only give me a chance. I will become the man you deserve. I love you with every cell in my body—more than life itself. I'd made up my mind to tell you, but

I was waiting for the right time. Again, that was my cowardice. But I wanted to tell you everything and beg for your forgiveness. I never meant to hurt you. Please give me another chance."

"You broke my heart, Colin. I have no forgiveness or hope left in me, because you ruined me. You stole my chance to choose you, and I'll never forgive you for that."

"I love you, Jihae. I'll never stop loving you."

Even if she didn't believe him, he had to try to convince her that she was loved and cherished by a foolish man. A fool's love was still love, and he hoped that it could provide her with a little salve for her pain. Colin got down on his knees in front of her, pulled out the ring from his pocket and held it out to her without opening the box.

"I won't insult you by even dreaming that you could accept my proposal, but once I told you everything, I was going to propose to you so I could spend the rest of my life loving you and making you happy. My love wasn't planned, but it's the greatest truth I know. And even if you can't accept me, please know that you are loved most deeply. Truly. Your father betrayed you, and I added to that hurt on the same day. My past mistakes are unforgivable, but causing you such pain today is beyond reprehensible. Please forget about me. Don't let your memory of me cause you any further pain. I'm not worth it."

Jihae didn't say a word, but tears were streaming down her face again, every drop like blood seeping from her heart. He got to his feet and placed the engagement ring on the counter.

"This is yours. There is no one else who will wear it. Do with it what you will." He turned from her then and took his first step toward the door and out of her life. But the burning pain in his heart made him turn around and look at her one last time. "I love you so very much. I'm sorry I couldn't be the man you deserve to be with."

It was only when he put his shaking hand on the doorknob that he heard her first broken sob. He held back the tears that rose to his eyes. He didn't deserve even a speck of relief from his anguish.

Thirteen

Time had passed. The cut on her palm had faded away into a thin white line, and Princes Jihae was able to pour herself into work without feeling much of anything. The production of *Best Placed Bets* was running toward the finish line. She was damn proud of what Rotelle Entertainment, CS Productions and the staff, crew and talent had accomplished.

Rule Two—they must finish the film no matter what—remained firmly in place, because she always kept her word. While she avoided Colin as much as humanly possible, her team continued to work with his to make the most of their partnership.

Every day she went to work and pushed herself to exhaustion, then came home and collapsed into a restless sleep. Every day. That was how she had survived the last few months.

In the rare moments that her guard came down and she remembered she'd lost Colin, pain too monstrous to describe came crashing into her, paralyzing her. But that just motivated her to fall deeper into character and become Princess Jihae down to her soul. It was a good thing. Everything she was—her face, body, hands and heart—all felt numb from the cold. She was frozen solid, and her true self remained locked behind the thick, icy walls.

The old Jihae had trusted, hoped and loved, but Princess Jihae knew better. Trust, hope and love only led to heartbreak. Her childish hope that her parents loved her despite their distance, censure and neglect... It was so stupid of her. Her dream that she could belong to someone and have that someone belong to her. To love and be loved. A complete joke. She was alone. She had always been and always would be. Alone.

"Hey, girlfriend. Do you have a minute?" June asked as she stepped into the office.

"For you. Anytime." Jihae did her best to smile for her friend. Her confidante. But it felt foreign and awkward on her face. "Come have a sit."

June held out a bag she had been hiding behind her back. "Ta-da."

A rusty, unnatural laugh rattled from her. "What is it?"

"*Nigiri*, baby. One of the staff went to Little Tokyo

for lunch and was sweet enough to bring some sushi back for us."

Jihae's stomach roiled, but she smiled her distant, stiff smile again. "How nice of them."

"Jihae-ya," June said, switching to Korean. "You really need to eat. You're going to make yourself sick pushing yourself like this."

"And since when do I not push myself?"

"I know. You always ask a lot of yourself, but not like this. I could tell you're not sleeping well, and you're wasting away. I hardly ever see you eat."

"I eat." When she remembered, which was seldom. "Okay, okay. Give me those *nigiri*. I'll eat them."

"Thank you, Your Majesty, for condescending to eat the gourmet sushi presented right in front of your face."

June's trademark sarcasm pulled free a real smile from Jihae. "Thank you for the sushi. And thank you for taking care of me."

"You're very welcome." She smiled back, relief shining on her face.

They ate in companionable silence, June piping up to make random, funny comments here and there. The sushi surprisingly wasn't dry and flavorless, like all the other food she'd attempted to eat. She could actually taste the fresh fish and the perfect texture of the rice, and it was delicious. A thin string of warmth penetrated her icy wall, and an impossible thought occurred to Jihae.

Maybe, just maybe, she would come out of this okay. Not whole and strong, but at least, as a *living* person. She had lost so much of herself from her father's betrayal and from Colin's... She'd lost Colin. She'd begun to think that she would never be herself again. That the real Jihae would never emerge from behind the wall of Princess Jihae.

But this could be the first step. The first real smile. The first enjoyable meal. The first time she enjoyed someone else's company since her world had collapsed. Maybe from this point on, she could take little steps to find herself again. To find satisfaction in her work, and to find whatever happiness she could find in her life.

"Thank you, June," she said with affection.

June's eyes widened in surprise and she smiled warmly at Jihae. "My absolute pleasure."

"We should do this again soon."

"Lunch? Nah. The next step to rehabilitation is getting you drunk."

"I like that idea. We could get plastered and go kill it at a karaoke."

"Now you're talking." June paused and looked straight into Jihae's eyes. "Welcome back, friend. I missed you so much."

The wrap party was one occasion when Jihae couldn't avoid Colin. They'd done the film together. He had as much right to be there as she did. She chose a loose, draping column dress to hide her weight loss and wore her hair down in thick, shiny waves. Possibly the only good thing that came out of the whole mess was that she didn't give a damn about what her father thought anymore.

He continued to threaten to fire her from her position for disobeying him, but he wasn't going to risk the financial success he stood to gain from *Best Placed Bets*. Her guess was he would push her out of Rotelle Entertainment as soon as the project was over. Jihae huffed a humorless laugh. Too bad she was leaving before he could have the satisfaction of firing her. She'd stuck with Rotelle Entertainment to see this film through, but she had plans to start her own production company.

The moment she entered the party, she was surrounded by people, so she didn't get a chance to see if Colin was there. It was for the best since she didn't want to spend the whole evening wondering if and when she would bump in to him.

Everyone in the grand hall was in high spirits. From the direction to the acting, everything had been superbly done in the film. They were filled with confidence that it would really be something to behold once the editing was finished. In her years in the industry, Jihae had never quite seen anything like it.

While she held herself to rigid standards, working on *Best Placed Bets* had been an absolute pleasure. They'd all worked together as a team through the rare minor hitches, but most of the production process had fallen into place like well-carved puzzle pieces. It was an uncommon but satisfying experience. And being part of it all had truly been an honor.

"Jihae," Ethan said, coming up to her with Kimberly beside him. "Congratulations. It has been an absolute pleasure to work with you."

"Ditto." Kimberly leaned in to hug her, and Jihae embraced her warmly.

"You guys did such wonderful jobs," Jihae said. "I can't tell you how proud I am, and how grateful I am that I had a chance to work with you both."

"Thank you, Jihae," Kimberly said with a watery smile. Then she cleared her throat. "Colin said he had a meeting, but he should be here any minute now."

"Oh?" Jihae couldn't think of anything to say beyond that.

The three of them weren't able to continue their conversation much longer as Jihae got pulled this way and that. When she was able to disentangle herself from the throngs of happy, celebrating colleagues, she made for the bar like a woman on a mission. Despite her mental preparations and determination, she was a nervous wreck at the prospect of seeing Colin.

"Dirty martini. Extra olives, please," she said to the bartender as she took an empty seat.

The others sitting at the bar seemed like the introverts of their group, seeking some alone time, which was perfect for her. She wanted to be alone with her beautiful martini for a few minutes. She took a sip of the bitter, briny cocktail and bit into the flesh of a salty olive. Her eyes closed shut. It was heavenly.

"Hennessy straight," said a voice she recognized from her dreams.

Why had he approached her? She'd expected an awkward hello, but she hadn't prepared herself to actually talk to Colin. She wasn't ready, so she kept her eyes closed and silently chewed her olive.

"Jihae."

Oh, God. She hated his beautiful voice. She hated the reflexive shiver that ran down her spine. She hated the thump of her broken heart. *Get a grip, Princess. You can do this.* She opened her eyes and slowly turned around. Colin was standing a few feet away, leaning against the bar.

"Congratulations on the wrap." She forced her words through stiff lips. He had worked hard and deserved the compliment.

"Thank you. Congratulations to you, too."

"Sure." She took a significant gulp of her martini.

Meanwhile, she was trying very hard not to notice anything about him. How striking he looked in his slim, black suit and open-necked dress shirt. How elegant his long fingers looked wrapped around his glass. He'd lost weight. His boyishly handsome face was now sharp and edgy. The face of a man who had known pain and survived. She tried to notice none of it. He wasn't hers anymore. Was never hers to begin with.

But she had something to relay to him, so she calmed her churning emotions.

"I want you to know that I've found some evidence connecting Rotelle Corporation to Yami. There were some suspicious activities in an overseas account belonging to one of Rotelle's shell companies. My father hid his tracks well, but some forensics showed the money being transferred to an account here. It isn't enough to put my father away, but it'll be enough to keep him from coming after Hansol Corporation and your family again. I'll make sure of that."

"Thank you, Jihae."

"No need to thank me. It's the right thing to do." Having said her piece, she was ready to find a dark hole to crawl into. She couldn't bear to be near Colin anymore.

"You look lovely," he said, his voice low and hesitant.

"Don't." Her numb frozen heart cracked and bled.

"Jihae, I just want to know that you're okay."

She froze as fury leaped to the surface. She couldn't believe what she was hearing. And she didn't want to believe the tenderness in his eyes.

"No, you don't get to see if I'm okay. What you get to do is stay away from me. I'm barely beginning to live again. You can't pop back into my life and ask after me. You forfeited that right when you destroyed me."

"I'm sorry. God, I didn't mean to… I'm an idiot. I'm sorry."

Enough. Jihae drained her drink and shot to her feet, but before she could storm off, Colin gave her a curt nod and strode off toward the opposite end of the hall. *God help me.* She wanted to run after him. Because despite everything, she still loved him with all her broken heart.

It was the night of Adelaide and Mike's wedding rehearsal. His cousin held a special place in his heart and she was marrying a man who actually deserved her. Colin was happy for them but the feeling was dull and faded.

His world was devoid of Jihae, and he was hollowed out. Life had lost its vitality, and he merely endured and survived it. Not that he deserved anything more. He'd betrayed her and broken her trust so completely, he couldn't even try to apologize to her again. He didn't deserve her forgiveness. For months, he'd tortured himself with thoughts of should've, could've, would've. He should have done a million things differently. Maybe then, he'd still have Jihae in his life.

But it was too late for regrets. He had poured all his energy into finishing the production of *Best Placed Bets*. At the very least, he'd kept that promise to her. Now he would have something they'd created together to hold on to. To keep him afloat in an existence he could hardly stand.

Colin was Mike's groomsman so his presence was mandatory, and there was no way he would ever let them down. Garrett and Natalie were the best man and the matron of honor respectively, so they had made the trip home from New York with their two daughters in tow. Colin's sorrow and anguish were his to bear, and it was time to take care of the people who loved him.

The wedding party bustled around the small chapel like tiny figurines in a shoebox. While everything seemed chaotic, Adelaide's wedding coordinator had the situation under tight control. If he remembered

Garrett and Natalie's wedding correctly, the woman was a genius at what she did.

He found Natalie standing near the edge of the commotion, holding an infant in her arms.

"Hey, there," he said, giving her a one-armed hug and a peck on her cheek. Then he stole a peek at the sleeping angel, just three months old. "Does she have superpowers? How is she sleeping through this ruckus?"

"Riley sleeps through anything as long as I'm holding her. But the moment I put her down in her car seat, she'll wake up in a second."

"May I hold her for a bit?"

"Oh, my God. Yes, please. My arms are burning," Natalie said as she gingerly transferred the little bundle into Colin's waiting arms. "You're a saint. Truly."

"And where is my dear cousin while you carry his daughter to the point of exhaustion?"

"Why, he's on the more difficult task of toddler duty." She laughed lightly and pointed past his head. "Look over there."

He spotted Garrett's tall, broad form easily, made all the more prominent by the three-year-old on his shoulders. His cousin was leaning his head toward Mike to hear what was being said, but the bellowing commands of his preschooler seemed to make it difficult for him. Colin chuckled quietly, shaking his head.

"So Sophie still rules the household, I see."

"Hey. That's only because I allow her to."

"What about Garrett?"

"Oh, no. He doesn't get to rule. He's putty in us women's hands."

Surprised laughter escaped his lips, and he worried he'd disturb the sleeping baby in his arms. Thankfully, Riley really could sleep through anything.

The rehearsal dinner was held on the Song family's garden terrace. After the harried wedding rehearsal, the setting was perfectly intimate and peaceful. When Adelaide's bridesmaids and Michael's bickering parents left, the cousins relaxed into the evening. His grandmother finally stood and bid everyone goodnight after a long, pointed look at Adelaide.

Garrett had put his two girls to bed at some point in the evening, and sat with his arm around his wife's shoulder. And Adelaide and Mike held hands on the table and cast blushing glances at each other. Never had Colin missed Jihae more than he did now.

"Will you please stop making those lost-puppy-dog eyes, Colin?" Adelaide said. "It makes me want to fuss over you and shower you with affection."

"Yeah. It's pretty damn heartbreaking," Garrett added.

"Screw you, dear cousins," Colin replied mildly. But he was panicking inside. Of course, his family would know. They could see his suffering as clearly as he could see their happiness.

"Hal-muh-nee debriefed us on your truly mucked up situation. I can see why she enlisted all of us to help. You're a mess, dear cousin," Adelaide said gently. "I think it's a Song family trait. When we fall in love, we love deeply. We love forever. You have to find a way to win her back."

"That's not possible. She would never forgive me. Nor should she." Colin gave up trying to maintain a light mood. They would see through him, anyway.

"Just look at me and Garrett, man," Mike chimed in. "We both messed things up so royally, we shouldn't be sitting at this table with these amazing women by our sides."

"But their capacity for love and forgiveness is greater than what we could possibly imagine," Garrett said, his voice rough with emotion. "And I don't know where I would be today if Natalie hadn't taken me back."

"Oh, honey." Natalie kissed Garrett softly on his mouth and leaned her head against his shoulder. "It was the best decision I ever made."

"Sometimes you have to forget about weighing things out, and just trust your gut instinct." Adelaide linked her fingers through Mike's. "If I hadn't taken a leap of faith, I wouldn't be the happy bride that I am."

"Are you happy, baby?" Mike asked her with such tenderness in his eyes. "Because that's all I ever wanted."

"I am. So happy." Adelaide cupped Mike's cheek in her hand and he leaned into it. "And I can't wait to start the rest of my life with you."

"God, could you guys all stop being so goddamn happy for a second?" Colin raked his fingers through his hair. He was pleased for his cousins, but it reminded him of what could've been. It hurt to think about Jihae. "I thought you guys were doing some kind of intervention for me. Not rubbing salt into my wounded heart with your love fest."

"We're just showing you what you could have if you got over your guilt and focus on your love," Adelaide said.

"What we've learned is that love makes us stupid brave. Maybe a little reckless, but mostly brave." Garrett smiled as though being stupid in love was the greatest thing in the world. "That bravery could help you do anything."

"What about the investigation?" Colin said, feeling terrifying hope spark to life inside him. "Aren't we going to bring charges against Rotelle Corporation and Chairman Park?"

"Bring charges against the devious devil himself? I wish," Garrett said. "But he was so thorough in covering up Rotelle's involvement that our PI ran out of leads again. And Sylvia Taylor hasn't made a peep. Jihae made it pretty clear that there will be no introduction to the talent agency, so she wisely gave up."

"Besides, Hansol discovered the espionage scheme before permanent harm could be done. And Natalie and Garrett are doing great. Right, guys?" Adelaide said, giving her brother and sister-in-law a big thumbs-up. "We could leave the past in the past, Colin. If you love Jihae, we'll stop the investigation against Rotelle Corporation. And I say this with Halmuh-nee's stamp of approval. We don't need to go after her family and hurt her."

"Do you love her?" Natalie asked gently.

"More than life," Colin replied. He loved Jihae so much that every cell in his body ached to hold her again.

"Then go win her back." Adelaide kicked him under the table. "Do the bravest, stupidest thing you can think of and overwhelm her with your love. She won't be able to think past her love for you."

"And we're all here to help you," Mike said. Everyone at the table nodded their support. "Just say the word and we'll do whatever you ask."

Emotion lodged itself in his throat, and Colin let himself weep for the first time after losing Jihae. But the tears were meant to cleanse away his guilt and regret, and prepare him to win back the woman he loved. Because if he knew anything, it was that he loved Jihae more than anything in the world and he would do everything in his power to make her happy. No matter what happened, he wanted her to know that he was hers and would always be hers. She deserved to know that his love was real.

Fourteen

Jihae checked into a hotel near the premiere location to get herself ready for the red carpet. Her stylist was scheduled to come in an hour. After a quick shower, She wrapped herself up in a plush bathrobe and dried her hair, absentmindedly running her fingers through it.

She'd chosen a warm, rose-and-gold dress for the occasion. She now only wore white when she damn well felt like wearing white. After the wrap party, she realized that if she wanted to survive, then she had to move on. And the first step had been to break free of her father's hold on her. Hiding behind Princess Jihae's persona was what was expected of her. She was not Princess Jihae. The princess belonged to her father. She had been a puppet controlled by her father. Never again.

She was Jihae Park, film producer and business executive. She was the one who had brought Rotelle Entertainment to the next level. That took skills, intelligence, perseverance and plain old hard work. After the premiere, she was going to submit a formal resignation letter to her father. It was time to devote herself to getting her production company off the ground. And with the evidence she had against Rotelle Corporation, her father wouldn't be able to do a damn thing to stop her.

The hollow, cold feeling where her heart used to be showed no signs of diminishing, but she couldn't let her life and happiness depend on another human being. It was no one's job to find happiness for her. It was hers and hers alone. She was still too ragged to feel whole, but she would find joy in her life, and make something of herself.

She wasn't a nobody just because her father saw fit to discard her like a used paper plate. She had been fooled by a man who claimed to love her, but she wasn't a fool for it. Someday, these things would make her stronger. It was too soon, but she would rise above everything she'd gone through.

There was a smart knock at the door, and she glanced at the clock. There were still at least forty minutes left until her appointment. Jihae walked to the door and looked out the peephole. It was June.

"June," she said, hugging her friend. "What are you doing here?"

"I pushed back your appointment for half an hour, so we have a good hour to talk."

"Talk? About what?"

"I don't know if this is going to change anything, but watching you put on a brave face every day hasn't been easy. You can't exist as a numb shell." June dragged Jihae to the settee and plopped both of them onto it. "You're a strong woman. You can fight. You can thrive. But will you ever be truly happy without Colin? Because I've never seen you light up from the inside out like when you were with Colin."

"Was it that obvious I was in love with him?"

"Honey, please." June waved her hand dismissively. "The way the two of you looked at each other fogged up the office windows."

"Why didn't you say anything?"

"About you two being together? Because you would have told me if it was something you wanted to share."

"It wasn't going to be anything permanent. I never thought—" A sob broke out against her will. She took deep breaths through her nose. She promised herself she wouldn't shed a single tear for Colin ever again.

"You never thought you would fall in love with him."

Jihae could only nod.

"Oh, hon. I think you guys fell for each other the first time you met." June reached out to squeeze her hand and held on to it in quiet support. "It's my job to be observant. I wouldn't be a good executive assistant if I wasn't. It was hard to ignore how lovesick you guys were."

"Colin doesn't love me. He—he was just using me."

"I know. You told me he kept his identity a secret from you and eavesdropped on your conversation with your father. That was a dick move on his part, but at least he was doing it for his family. And that gets me to the part why I rushed over here."

"What is it?" Jihae asked, unable to quell her curiosity.

"It's about Colin's relationship with his family. It wasn't only you. No one knows about his connection to the Song family and Hansol. He has kept it a tightly held secret all his life."

"How did you find that out?"

"Colin's cousin Adelaide called me a few days ago. She said she didn't know if you would take her call, so she reached out to me. Colin must've told her I was your friend. Someone you would listen to."

"But why are you telling me this now?"

"You're trying so hard to put your life back together. I didn't know if telling you would only make things harder for you. But no. You love him, and you have a right to see the whole picture."

June explained that his father had coasted through a life of privilege and entitlement on his family's money and good name. He was hardly a father to Colin. It was his grandmother, Grace Song, who had raised him.

But as he grew older, Colin was desperate to make

his name and succeed on his own outside the shadow of Hansol. He didn't want to be anything like his father. In order to become a self-made man, he closely guarded his identity from the public. He refused to benefit from his connections. But in order to stand on his own, he had to disappoint his grandmother and refuse to join Hansol.

"I know this doesn't excuse him from not telling you he was Garrett Song's cousin, but everything in him must have rebelled against revealing his secret. He didn't even know if he could trust you to keep his identity a secret, so he had gone with his default. Just like in any situation, he would have wanted to be judged based on the merits rather than his connections and his family name."

Jihae didn't need to hear this right now. She didn't want to know that he was an honest, honorable man. That he had to bear the guilt of disappointing the person who'd raised him to be true to himself. When the opportunity arose to allow him to help his family, how could he refuse? No. She couldn't do this right now. She couldn't feel her heart wrench for the little boy Colin was, and for the man he became. She didn't want to feel the tears streaking down her cheeks.

"I'm not telling you this to hurt you, Jihae. You are fierce and amazing, and I'm so proud of you. But I don't want you to have any regrets. His motivations don't make his actions right, but maybe it'll help you look at what happened in a less punishing light. Maybe it'll help you hurt less to know that what he did wasn't a coldhearted scheme."

Jihae abruptly stood from her seat, and wiped her tears away with both hands. "June, thank you for rushing here to tell me all this. You're a good friend, and I love you for it."

"But?"

"But I'm going to kick you out now because I have a premiere to get ready for and I don't want my face to be a swollen mess. I can't deal with this right now."

"You know he'll be there tonight."

"Of course, I know. All the more reason I can't show up with puffy, red eyes. I don't want him to think that I'm still crying over him. Let me keep a scrap of dignity in all this. I won't have to see him ever again after this."

"That. I just needed to make sure *that* was what you still wanted after learning the full story." June gathered her jacket and got on her feet. "I think my work here is done, and I will bid you adieu."

"Thank you, June."

"Have a wonderful night. You earned this, and *Best Placed Bets* is going to blow everyone away."

After one last hug, June left Jihae to her thoughts. But she kept her mind carefully blank even as her heart pumped and churned inside her, water raining down from her heart as the ice around it melted.

Jihae arrived near the end of the line for the red carpet. The stylist had chastised her repeatedly for her tears, and it had taken ages to make her look presentable. When she stepped out of the car, flash bulbs burst around her, and she gave them her real smile, rather than her signature Princess Jihae half smile. Despite everything, she was proud to be there, and proud of the film she'd produced.

She heard the expected chatter over the color of her dress and her free-flowing hair. Even her makeup was warm and stormy, unlike her former icy, elegant looks. Appearing before the public as herself was incredible. It freed something inside her. The insecurities and resentment she carried deep within unchained themselves and flew away. She was here as her own person, and she was fiercely proud of who she was.

She stopped and smiled for the cameras for what seemed like the hundredth time when she heard a commotion behind her. From her perch on the stairs, she saw a small group of people walking toward her and the crowd parted like red curtains to allow them through. At that moment, she spotted the tall, broad-shouldered man wearing a velvet, royal blue tuxedo. She thought anyone would have been able to single him out of the crowd, even the Hollywood red-carpet crowd.

He looked exquisitely handsome with his slightly unruly hair slicked back from his forehead. He was even thinner than when she'd last seen him, but he looked sharp and sophisticated…and full of determination. Colin had always been a confident man with an air of authority about him even as his usual, lighthearted self. But the man who stood on the carpet looked like he was ready to take on the world, exuding power from every part of him.

When he came to stand at the bottom of the short staircase, Jihae realized she'd been holding her breath. She let it out in a rush and stretched out her hand to steady herself on the rail.

"Jihae." His voice was low and tense, but hearing her name from his lips sent a thrill down her spine. "You look so beautiful."

"Colin, what are you doing?" she said, glancing around at the gathering crowd.

"I just wanted you to know how much I love you." His voice broke. "I know I've hurt you—so much—because of my guilty conscience and hang-ups. I've betrayed—"

"Stop that." Jihae rushed down the steps and tugged him to the side until they were a few feet away from the red carpet. It didn't exactly give them privacy, but the reporters had now turned to the next celebrity walking down the carpet.

"I've betrayed your trust," he continued as though there was no interruption. "I've invaded your privacy by eavesdropping on you. And most of all, I should've believed in you and trusted you with my truth."

"Colin, we're done. You've apologized already and I've declined to accept." She tried to sound aloof and disinterested, but her voice shook.

The thought of him as a little boy without a father he could look up to, and of him as a young man, disappointing the woman who raised him to become the man he was today… It tore at her heart.

"I love you so much and I was so afraid of losing you that I was slowly losing my mind. I fooled myself into thinking that I could let you go when the time came. I tried to convince myself that what we had was a brief affair and no one would get hurt. I told myself to cherish every day with you because it was bound to end. That telling you the truth was only bound to hurt you."

His confession made her realize how she had tried to fool herself in the same way. She'd told herself she could keep herself from falling in love with him. She had always planned on leaving him. Foolishly believed that she would be able to leave him. She lied to herself to protect her heart, but Colin had still given his heart to her. He had loved her all along, and had fought with the fear and guilt inside him.

"I don't know if I could believe you. You broke my heart, Colin."

"I know I did. God, I know. But losing you broke me. Nothing has meaning to me anymore. Please give me a chance to love you. I will dedicate my life to making it up to you. To making you happy. Without you, my world is colorless."

A sob escaped her. Her life as Princess Jihae had been colorless. *She* had been colorless, lifeless, until she met Colin. He had filled her life with color, and she was finally able to bring out all the beautiful, powerful colors within herself. And she wanted so much to forgive him. To grab the happiness he was offering her. But she was so afraid.

"I don't think I could endure another broken heart. I won't be able to survive next time." Tears ran down her face, probably undoing all the hard work of her stylist, but it was hopeless. There was no way she could stem her tears.

"I swear to you there will never be a next time. I will never keep a secret from you again. I'm far from perfect, and I may hurt you at times in my stupidity, but I will always own up to it and work harder to be the man you deserve. Please." Colin kneeled before her on the cold asphalt. "Please give me a chance to love you. Let me cherish you for the rest of our lives."

Jihae was so entranced by Colin's words that she didn't see the group of people who came to stand behind him for a second. Then she drew back in shock. It was the Song family. She recognized Garrett Song and Grace Song from the business papers, and Adelaide Song from the fashion magazines. James Song was also there. Another man and woman stood beside Adelaide and Garrett, and seemed to be their significant others. They all wore warm smiles and earnest expressions. All but Grace Song, who stood in the middle with calm dignity.

"Please forgive him," James Song said. "He's so entertaining."

"We'll personally kick his ass if he misbehaves again," Garrett said as though he meant it.

"He's an idiot but we love him." Adelaide shrugged. "Could you, too?"

Then Mrs. Song finally spoke. "Will you be a part of our family?"

"Will you give me another chance?" Colin asked, still kneeling in front of her with tears brimming in his eyes.

He had always kept his connection to his family a closely guarded secret. But he had enlisted all their help to win her back. Her tears fell furiously. He had done this for her. Despite the scar in his heart left by his father, Colin wanted to open himself up to her, and in doing so, revealed to the world that he was Colin Song of the Hansol Song family.

"You just revealed your secret in public." She stated the obvious, too awed to be clever.

"I know. I don't care who knows. This secret I'd held on to for so long was merely a form of my pride. I wanted to be seen for the man I was, and I wanted to claim my success as my own. But all my life, my family has been there for me, and I couldn't have done anything without their love and support."

"Oh, Colin."

"And I offer you not only my love and support, but my family's as well. Will you marry me and grant me—us—the privilege of being your family?"

"Yes," she whispered then said with more strength, "Yes, I will marry you, Colin Song. Please stand up."

He stood and pulled a small box out of his pocket. It was the one she had messengered back to him. He carefully withdrew the diamond ring, and asked, "May I?"

"Yes."

He lifted her hand and pushed the ring onto her finger. It fit perfectly. When she glanced toward the Song family, Adelaide and Garrett's wife were wearing tremulous, watery smiles, and even the men's eyes were red-rimmed. She looked toward Grace Song and she gave her a solemn nod with a gentle smile on her face. They were going to be a family.

"You're mine now, you know." Colin raised her hand and kissed her softly on the knuckles, smoothing his thumbs over the ring. "And you can't back out because we have a ton of witnesses."

Jihae had been so focused on Colin and his family that she didn't realize that they were again surrounded by cameras...and applause.

"Oh, well." She cupped his cheek, all her love shining in her eyes. "I guess I'm stuck."

"You bet you are." Colin dipped her back to the roar of their audience and kissed her thoroughly, marking the beginning of their happily ever after.

* * * * *

*Don't miss
a single story in
The Heirs of Hansol series
by Jayci Lee!*

Temporary Wife Temptation
Secret Crush Seduction
Off Limits Attraction

*Available exclusively
from Harlequin Desire*

**WE HOPE YOU ENJOYED
THIS BOOK FROM**

⬡ HARLEQUIN
DESIRE

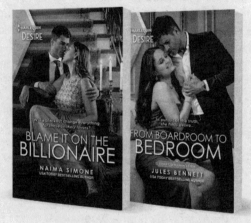

*Luxury, scandal, desire—welcome to
the lives of the American elite.*

Be transported to the worlds of oil barons, family dynasties,
moguls and celebrities. Get ready for juicy plot twists,
delicious sensuality and intriguing scandal.

6 NEW BOOKS AVAILABLE EVERY MONTH!

Cricket Maxfield had a hell of a hand. And her confidence made
that clear. Poor little thing didn't think she needed a poker face if
she had a hand that could win.

But he knew better.

She was sitting there with his hat, oversize and over her eyes, on
her head and an unlit cigar in her mouth.

A mouth that was disconcertingly red tonight, as she had clearly
conceded to allowing her sister Emerson to make her up for the
occasion. That bulky, fringed leather jacket should have looked
ridiculous, but over that red dress, cut scandalously low, giving a
tantalizing wedge of scarlet along with pale, creamy cleavage, she
was looking not ridiculous at all.

And right now, she was looking like far too much of a winner.

Lucky for him, around the time he'd escalated the betting, he'd
been sure she would win.

He'd wanted her to win.

"I guess that makes you my ranch hand," she said. "Don't worry.
I'm a very good boss."

Now, Jackson did not want a boss. Not at his job, and not in his
bedroom. But her words sent a streak of fire through his blood. Not
because he wanted her in charge. But because he wanted to show
her what a boss looked like.

Cricket was…

A nuisance. If anything.

That he had any awareness of her at all was problematic enough. Much less that he had any awareness of her as a woman. But that was just because of what she was wearing. The truth of the matter was, Cricket would turn back into the little pumpkin she usually was once this evening was over and he could forget all about the fact that he had ever been tempted to look down her dress during a game of cards.

"Oh, I'm sure you are, sugar."

"I'm your boss. Not your sugar."

"I wasn't aware that you winning me in a game of cards gave you the right to tell me how to talk."

"If I'm your boss, then I definitely have the right to tell you how to talk."

"Seems like a gray area to me." He waited for a moment, let the word roll around on his tongue, savoring it so he could really, really give himself all the anticipation he was due. "Sugar."

"We're going to have to work on your attitude. You're insubordinate."

"Again," he said, offering her a smile, "I don't recall promising a specific attitude."

There was activity going on around him. The small crowd watching the game was cheering, enjoying the way this rivalry was playing out in front of them. He couldn't blame them. If the situation wasn't at his expense, then he would have probably been smirking and enjoying himself along with the rest of the audience, watching the idiot who had lost to the little girl with the cigar.

He might have lost the hand, but he had a feeling he'd win the game.

Don't miss what happens next in…
The Rancher's Wager
by New York Times *bestselling author Maisey Yates!*

Available January 2021 wherever
Harlequin Desire books and ebooks are sold.

Harlequin.com

HDEXP1220

Love Harlequin romance?

DISCOVER.

Be the first to find out about promotions, news and exclusive content!

Facebook.com/HarlequinBooks

Twitter.com/HarlequinBooks

Instagram.com/HarlequinBooks

Pinterest.com/HarlequinBooks

ReaderService.com

EXPLORE.

Sign up for the Harlequin e-newsletter and download a free book from any series at **TryHarlequin.com**

CONNECT.

Join our Harlequin community to share your thoughts and connect with other romance readers!
Facebook.com/groups/HarlequinConnection

HSOCIAL2020